The Cat That Wasn't There

Stella Whitelaw

A SIGNET BOOK

SIGNET
Published by the Penguin Group
Penguin Books USA Inc., 375 Hudson Street,
New York, New York 10014, U.S.A.
Penguin Books Ltd, 27 Wrights Lane,
London W8 5TZ, England
Penguin Books Australia Ltd, Ringwood,
Victoria, Australia
Penguin Books Canada Ltd, 10 Alcorn Avenue,
Toronto, Ontario, Canada M4V 3B2
Penguin Books (N.Z.) Ltd, 182–190 Wairau Road,
Auckland 10, New Zealand

Penguin Books Ltd, Registered Offices:
Harmondsworth, Middlesex, England

First published in the United States by Signet, an imprint of New Amer-
ican Library, a division of Penguin Books USA Inc. Previously published
in Great Britain by Grafton Books, under the title *New Cat Stories*.

First Signet Printing, June, 1992
10 9 8 7 6 5 4 3 2 1

REGISTERED TRADEMARK—MARCA REGISTRADA

Printed in the United States of America

PUBLISHER'S NOTE
These are works of fiction. Names, characters, places, and incidents
either are the product of the author's imagination or are used ficti-
tiously, and any resemblance to actual persons, living or dead, events,
or locales is entirely coincidental.

To B.S.

adviser on things electrical
and atmospheric

CONTENTS

THE CAT THAT WASN'T THERE

No one knew about the cat that lived in the roof. He had a clever way of getting in, discovered on a day when a sudden downpour caught him on the edge of the steeply sloping north elevation. He clung, blinded and battered, on a perilous corner, unable to see to go either forwards or backwards.

He was about ten months old then, a strong young cat, half wild but already wise in the ways of surviving in an alien world.

He hung on to the roof, unable to see, the rain gluing his eyelids together; hardly able to breathe as gusts of wind knocked the air out of his slender ribcage. He dared not jump or consider movement in any direction. In moments his crew-cut black fur flattened to a second skin, his long tail saturated to become a skinny rope hanging in mid-air.

His nose sniffed a whiff of dry dust. It was this sense which saved his life for he could not have held on much longer. Somewhere near this torrential exposure to water was an oasis of dryness if only he could find it. He peered through slit eyes at the weathered eighteenth-century tiling that surrounded him.

There was a diagonal crack across one tile and the broken triangle had slipped. Carefully be eased himself along the gutter, sniffing. He had no idea where the inch-wide crack might lead, if anywhere at all. It might simply be a dead end, stuffed with an abandoned swallow's nest.

He nosed at the crack, its sharp edges scratching the tender skin. It moved. He tried again while the wind battered and buffeted at him as if he were an old shuttlecock. He gathered the muscles in his shoulders and pushed in desperation. Why should anything save him? his senses questioned. He was nothing, exposed to everything, a cat denied even the most meager of comforts—a scrap of food, shelter, a wet hole.

The capricious wind rooted on his side for six solitary seconds.

It was enough. The force of the wind gathered under the tile to shift it another inch. Then a different, malicious gust took the broken half and threw it down into the courtyard with a great burst of temper.

The cat clung to the guttering, claws slipping,

back arched, ears flattened. Then, fast as a black snake, he slithered into the gap under the roof.

It was hollow, just large enough for the cat to curl into and blink the rain out of his eyes. The loose tile above shuddered in distress, but it kept him dry. It could make as much noise as it liked, as long as it stayed put.

Gradually the cat's erratic pulse quietened and the tenseness dropped out of his limbs. The black void reminded him of a cozy, warm, pre-birth existence where he had been safe. He slept, exhausted.

He was awoken by drips on his nose. The storm had died down and the rearguard rivulets were draining off the roof. He retreated a few inches, offended by the cooling drops on his dry fur.

There was an emptiness behind him as he edged himself backwards, trying not to imagine ravines and cliff edges and sheer drops into the courtyard. Eventually the channel widened and he was able to twist and turn round. His keen eyes saw weathered beams and rafters, centuries of builders' rubble. He was inside the roof of the house itself. He stretched his cramped limbs. He had never been in a house before. It seemed a paradise, warm and dry and spacious. He smelt mice and birds and his nose twitched in anticipation. Did any other cat own this delectable place?

By the end of two weeks he was glorying in his absolute reign of the rafters. He scuttled in and out with the dexterity of a tightrope walker. He had even managed to climb back into his sanctuary with a field mouse clamped in his jaws. He did not want to eat all his rafter mice at one go. They were his living, breeding larder. He was saving them for a rainy day.

One day he went further inside than he had ever ventured before, down a disused chimney. He found himself on another floor amid a clutter of furniture and boxes and cases, piles of old pictures, coal scuttles, umbrellas and cricket pads. He was bewildered. He did not understand what this place was. There were no humans though it smelt of long-ago people.

The only inhabitants were spiders and flies. He crunched a fly thoughtfully. Although the attic had interest value, it was not going to be a fruitful hunting ground. There was nothing to eat. But he did find a pile of old rugs and clothes that made the most luxurious bed. He trampled them into an acceptable shape and went to sleep.

Later he explored still further, finding a gap in the floorboards to squeeze through. He climbed steadily downwards like a mountaineer, using the wooden lathes as clawholds, easing himself down a narrow, dark cavity.

His small, enquiring nose met a wall of metal that exuded waves of heat. It was overpowering. It almost knocked him off his feet. Whatever was it? Had he come across a new kind of fire without flames?

He found a slim gap beneath the hot metal and wriggled through. If he had thought the rafters a paradise then this must be heaven itself. His paws sank and clawed into the soft pile of a carpet, reveling in the new experience. He sniffed and investigated all the bright toys littering the carpet; he patted a wobbly orange soldier and a small red ball. He found a tray with spilt milk and half-eaten biscuits, which he eagerly finished up.

He jumped up on to the bed, marveling at its amazing softness and warmth. Then he smelt human—small, clean and milk-sweet.

The black cat froze, alarmed, and turned into a shadow. Humans were totally unknown.

Nothing happened. The small human slept on, the blue teddy bears on his pyjamas rising and falling with his light breathing.

The cat trod nearer, carefully, curious to view this creature at close quarters. The boy stirred, flung an arm across the cat, plump fingers skimming the velvety black fur.

"P . . . ssy," he murmured.

The cat stayed till dawn creaked through the shutters. Then he thought he had better go while he was still safe. He squeezed under the radiator, climbed the interior wall partition, then, via the attic, found the way back to the roof. He was disturbed by his encounter with the small human. No one had ever spoken to him before. It had been . . . nice.

Henrietta was at her wits' end to know what to do about her small son, Giles. She was determined that he should be able to say at least a few words before her husband returned from his business trip to the States. They were both worried about their son, wondering if there had been brain damage at a forceps birth, despite assurances from the Harley Street obstetricians that they had a fine healthy son.

"He'll talk when he wants to talk," they told Henrietta.

Henrietta was not reassured. "Drinkie. Say *drinkie*, Giles," she said, offering him a mug of orange juice.

Giles grinned enchantingly and took the mug with both hands. There was nothing wrong with his co-ordination.

"Drinkie. Say *drinkie, please, Mummy*."

He looked up from the mug, his mouth moist and orange-rimmed. "P . . . ssy," he said.

His mother gave him an encouraging smile and a sponge finger. "Say *biccy. Biccy*, Giles."

He crumbled the sponge all over the floor. "P . . . ssy."

"No, no, no, Giles. Not on the floor. Say *sorry, Mummy*."

He rocked in his chair, grinning toothily. "P . . . ssy," he chanted.

Henrietta ran her hands through her hair. "I shall go mad. I *am* going mad!" She repeated the same conclusion on the telephone to Rupert that evening. "I read to him, talk to him, show him pictures, but he won't say a thing, not a word. He won't talk, he just won't talk. He only makes this awful hissing noise at me."

"Don't worry, darling. He's not two years old yet. Lots of children are not talking at two. He'll talk soon. It's not the right time for him yet; he's not ready."

That night the cat crept closer to the small

human, not afraid any more. Giles curled up and lay his head against the soft fur for a pillow. "P . . . ssy," he said contentedly.

Henrietta took Giles to a reputable children's speech therapist. She explained the child's resistance to words and his insistence on making this strangely explosive hissing sound. Giles wandered round the consulting room on sturdy legs, looking at everything with bright inquisitive eyes. He caught sight of all the stuffed animals on the windowsill and climbed up to reach one. He pulled down a fat gray elephant.

"P . . . ssy," he said triumphantly.

"No, Giles," said the therapist. "That's an elephant. E . . . le . . . phant."

"P . . . ssy," Giles insisted, but the corners of his mouth began to turn down.

"There you are, see?" said Henrietta. "He's hopeless. He just won't talk. Whatever am I going to do?"

"I can see you have a problem . . . Try speaking to him in his own language." The therapist peered closely at Giles. "Psst! Psst!"

Giles looked at him blankly, then solemnly gave back the elephant. "P . . . ssy," he said in a sad voice, shaking his head. "P . . . ssy."

The cat patted the bricks and balls and soldiers while Giles clapped his hands with delight. Then the cat finished off the milk in the cup, the biscuit crumbs from the plate, cleaning his milk-drenched whiskers with fastidious paws.

Giles climbed off his bed and crawled along

the carpet, making encouraging hand signals. The cat watched him cautiously. No one had ever touched him. Small human moving was vastly different from small human asleep.

Giles stroked him with careful, enquiring hands, making sweet crowing noises. The cat quivered under the inexpert, untutored caresses. "P ... ssy?" said Giles hopefully.

There was no improvement in Giles's speech before Rupert returned from his trip to the States. He found his wife pacing the house in a state of nerves.

"He must have brain damage," she cried. "I know it. Daddy was right. I can't get him to say anything."

"Your father knows nothing," said Rupert sternly. "Leave him out of this."

"Say *hello* to Daddy," Henrietta implored her son, pushing him towards Rupert, desperation sharpening her voice.

Giles viewed the strange dark man towering above him and clamped his mouth shut.

"Hello, Giles."

Giles wondered who the tall man could be. 'P ... ssy," he said eventually.

"There you are!" Henrietta shrieked. "I told you! That's all he does all day long."

Rupert felt sorry for the small boy hovering close by his mother's side. The toddler was almost a stranger to him; he had changed a lot in three months.

"It sounded remarkably like 'pussy' to me," he said.

"Nonsense. We haven't got a cat. You know I don't like them."

"But he might have heard the word somewhere, seen it in a book or something."

"Rubbish. Never. He says it to everything. It means nothing. He's besotted by the sound."

Rupert went down on one knee and regarded the bright eyes so similar to his own. He was not used to talking to small boys. Financial tycoons and advertising executives were more his style. "Pussy," he said experimentally.

Giles's face lit up like a beacon. He climbed enthusiastically over Rupert's well-pressed trousers. "P . . . ssy," he agreed.

Rupert sat back on his heels and wondered how he could console his distraught wife. "Don't get so upset," he said. "Perhaps Giles is going to be a vet."

One night the cat ventured still further through the nursery door, which had been left ajar. He slipped silently down the wide stairs and across the hall, into a big clean place that was teeming with tantalizing smells.

He nosed open the lid of a bin and pulled out the carcass of a whole chicken. He was astonished. What an odd place to keep a chicken. He chewed some meat, then rainy-day thoughts intruded and he knew he must hide his prize. His thought process was the same for a whole chicken as a surplus field mouse.

He dragged the chicken across the floor, up the stairs, along the landing, through Giles's bedroom, then somehow forced pieces under the radiator. He took his bounty up into the rafters. It lasted him for days. About as long as Henrietta took having hysterics, telling off the cook and making the maid scrub every inch of floor and shampoo the carpets.

Giles looked on all the activity with interest. At least his mother was not cross with him for the mess. "P . . . ssy," he said.

A man came to the door and offered to take photographs of their interesting old house. He would then make prints, gloss or matt, and put them in card holders, and they could send them to their friends as highly personalized Christmas cards. Henrietta was delighted by the offer; Rupert wasn't. He hated the idea.

Henrietta won and the man spent an hour taking photographs of their house from every angle. Ten days later he brought round the proofs for them to choose which view was the most flattering for their card. Rupert surveyed them with dismay. He liked his old house, but not on a Christmas card. He preferred holly and robins. He gave the pile of proofs to Giles to play with on the floor.

"P . . . ssy," said Giles tenderly, a look of utter devotion shining on his small face.

Rupert took the photograph away from his son and looked at it carefully. It was an angled shot of the roof, showing the interesting elevations and Elizabethan chimneys. He got a magnifying glass and peered more closely.

On a corner of the top roof, almost invisible against the shadows, sat a beautiful sleek black cat. It was so perfectly poised it could have been a statue or a weather vane; a good-luck mascot carved by some medieval stonemason.

Giles leaned on his father's shoulder, sticky hands gripping his white collar. One chubby, grubby finger pointed at the solitary black cat.

"P . . . ssy," said Giles adoringly.

"Your pussy?" asked his father. "Giles's pussy? Is that your cat? Giles's pussy?"

Giles grinned, wriggling. "Gi . . . es's p . . . ssy," he said.

Rupert sat back on his heels with relief. His son was not brain-damaged. He could talk. He was just taking his time. He would speak when he had something to say. And there must be a real cat somewhere, for Rupert knew that there was no statue on the roof.

It was the cat who saw the burglars climbing over the roof. They were shadows at first, long and unreal, spreading across the tiles like snakes. Panic hit the cat. If they found his secret way into the rafters then he would be lost, his home would be lost, his small human would be lost. Security, friendship, warmth, comfort, food . . . his life would end.

He threw back his head and howled loudly. It was the screech of a banshee. It echoed across the tiles, bouncing off the roof and hitting the walls with a desperation born of the wild.

Giles woke up and began to cry. Lights went on all over the house. Soon a blaze of lights beamed across the courtyard. Rupert hurried out and immediately spotted the men's shapes, crouching high on the roof. He removed their ladder and phoned for the police.

"Has anyone been taking photos of your house recently, sir?" said the police sergeant some time later, as the men were taken away.

"As a matter of fact, they have," said Rupert. "For Christmas cards."

"Thought so. We know this lot. They like to reconnoiter a place first. They've done a lot of houses round here. I wonder if I can have the photos as evidence?"

"Of course. All except one," said Rupert. "My son is rather fond of a particular view of his cat on the roof."

Giles looked up, hugging the photo close to his chest. He had just learned how to wink. It was a devastating new skill which he used on every occasion.

"Cat," he said quite clearly, with an outrageous wink.

I have always thought communication between myself and my mistress to be a little on the sparse side, not to say downright misleading at times. Of course, I understand her instantly, every word, honestly. It's either "Do this" or "Do that" or "Come here" or "Stop it, this very minute, you bad cat."

But she doesn't understand me at all. I don't always want something to eat, or to go out or come in like a furry yo-yo. It's far more complex. Perhaps I am reminding her to cook the frozen liver she brought home for my supper, then suddenly I'm whisked out of the door. Or I may be pointing out that the central heating is switched off and she'll ask me if I want a drink of milk. Most unsatisfactory, even hopeless at times, as you can imagine.

21

No one believes that I do have other things on my mind besides eating and drinking and traipsing in and out of her neat little house. My brain is seething with interesting information I long to impart. I could be telling her that the latest man in her life is a perfect drip, or that her new perfume is made from the musk of the cat family; but does she understand? No. I don't rate asking for more jellymeat Whiskas as conversation.

It is my burning ambition to communicate logically with Meryl and rid myself of this frustrating lack of expression. She means a lot to me, and despite excessive purring, pawing, etc., I'm not at all sure that she knows of my devotion.

Meryl spends a lot of time working for the letterbox. Very odd. She types black words on white paper and puts them in a brown envelope, which is then inserted into the red letterbox across the road. A colorful occupation but seemingly pointless. I always walk along the road with her to make sure she does not get lost on the way back.

"More work!" she says as the envelope goes through the slot.

I have spent many hours perched on top of the letterbox, watching and waiting. I don't understand why this letterbox swallows Meryl's work. I've tried looking inside but there's nothing at all happening down there. It's just an incredibly gloomy hole.

She also does daily "bread and butter" work, which entails rushing round like a demented rabbit in the morning, and then running down the road. Running down the road, I ask you! It doesn't make sense.

"I'm going to be late for work," she gasps, slinging me out into the garden.

"Meow'll run down the road for you," I offer, but she just waves goodbye and hurries along the pavement, buttoning her coat and putting on her gloves.

It's all mysterious and not proper work, to my mind. Not like guarding the house, keeping those yappy dogs at bay, chasing wasps off the fruit tree and letting the birds know who is boss. Now that's proper work. I'm often totally exhausted by my labors and barely have the strength to crawl on to Meryl's knee for my evening snooze.

One day a new machine appears on Meryl's desk and that noisy non-stop clatter-bang typewriter thing is banished to its rightful place at the back of the cupboard. This new machine is fascinating; it has a little sparkly white dancer which jumps around on a green face. I can watch it for hours.

"Meo .. r .. yl?" I ask, wanting to know what it is.

"Don't touch, Charlie," she warns. "This has cost me a fortune. It's the very latest technology.

I keep my distance, waiting and watching, all sorts of ideas buzzing round in my head. Meryl calls it a word processor. I know that words are to do with communication, and what I long for most in this world is to communicate with my young mistress.

At first she is very careful with the machine, always switching it off when she goes out of the room to answer the phone or make a cup of coffee, and putting a cover over the knobbly keyboard that she taps. But gradually she gets more confident about the machine and leaves its green face on and the little white dancer flashing and blinking impatiently for her return.

The first time she leaves it on, I leap on to her desk and put my nose close up to the tiny dancer. It does not smell, nor does it go away. It blinks at me curiously. What joy . . . I've found a friend! I pat the knobs tentatively with a paw and the little dancer pops up somewhere else and new black marks appear on the screen. This is fun . . . I walk over the keys and the dancer whirls like a demon. There seems to be a connection between my walking and the marks that appear.

I hear Meryl returning and in a flash I'm on the windowsill, staring blankly at a glossy blackbird pecking for worms in the lawn.

"Heavens," she says. "What's all this? My typing must be getting worse."

The next time I play with the dancer, it is even more fun. All four paws prancing at the same time sends it absolutely wild, whizzing all over the place. But Meryl is not so happy.

"Oh dear," she says on her return. "What on earth has happened? It's gone berserk."

She pores over a big hinged book called a manual, fretting and frowning, but to no avail. She's almost in tears till she finds something called a Rescue Service for WP Users in the yellow pages and rings them up. Later in the day a pleasant young man wearing glasses arrives at the house. He is very patient and sorts it all out.

"You overloaded your disc, then gave it the command to print when there was no free space to take the new edited version. You should have moved another file on to Drive M, then retrieved it after printing out," he explains.

Meryl nods hopefully, trying to understand the complexities of the jargon.

"Then for some reason you tried to initiate a totally new file when the program was still in print. That's why the screen flashed Error - File in Edit. Er . . . do you follow me?"

"I don't actually remember doing any of that," says Meryl humbly. "It's all news to me. But if you say I did, then I must have."

"Writer's block," says the rescuer, giving me a nice firm stroke along my spine as he goes out. There is nothing wishy-washy about this young man. "Bye, Charlie," he adds.

"How did you know his name?" Meryl asks.

"I thought all handsome gray tabbies answered to Charlie," he says with a wink to me.

The next day, Meryl has to phone him again. "I must have a rogue machine," she says with rising panic. "A whole lot of gibberish has suddenly appeared in the middle of a chapter I was writing. It's absolute rubbish. Listen to this, Mr. Richards. I insist on reading it to you."

I listen too.

" 'Dr. Roger Cavendish arrived early at the hospital so that he could guard the premises, chase noisy dogs out of the garden and keep the wasps from the fruit trees.' " Meryl pauses. "I didn't write any of that, really I didn't. Dr. Cavendish is my hero, a brain surgeon. He wouldn't be guarding the premises. It's just nonsense. It doesn't make sense."

Mr. Richards is obviously thinking. I jump on to the telephone table and put my head close to Meryl's ear. These disembodied voices coming from the air just fascinate me.

"Sounds a reasonable sentence to me," says Mr. Richards's voice. "But then I'm a computer expert not a literary critic. I don't think it's anything to do with your machine. Do you really need a service call? This could get expensive."

"No," she sighs, "I'll just delete the rubbish and start again. I must be working too hard. I've a deadline to meet."

My whiskers twitch. Rubbish indeed ... I think it is pretty good myself.

"Perhaps you ought to take some time off," he suggests. "After all, you're trying to cope with two jobs at once. Do you have to do all this writing? Why not go out, see a film ... relax."

"I can't. I haven't time."

I try to tell Meryl that Mr. Richards is quite right. She ought to take some time off and go out, preferably with Mr. Richards. But Meryl misunderstands me as usual and the next minute I am out in the garden and in an eye-to-eye confrontation with that damned blackbird.

Twenty-four hours later Meryl is convinced her machine is jinxed. She insists that William

Richards make a house call, despite it being the weekend.

"Look," she says in despair, scrolling the screen to her current piece of work. "I think I'm going mad. Read this . . . 'Sue Arnold took the first opportunity to spend her unexpected windfall in Bond Street. She bought half a pound of liver, a fillet of cod, a carton of cream and a packet of choc-o-drops.' I never wrote that; it's crazy writing." Her voice rises in hysteria. "Fillet of cod, I ask you. She's supposed to be an heiress!"

"Perhaps this heiress has a practical turn of mind," says William Richards, checking the computer. "Nothing seems to be wrong with your machine. Choc-o-drops, eh?"

A little quiver goes up and down my spine. I know the choc-o-drops are a mistake. Perhaps heiresses don't eat chocolates. And that William Richards is too smart. He is looking at me over the top of his glasses.

"Has your cat got a sweet tooth?" he asks.

I feel myself being transported rapidly mid-air in a strong pair of arms and put down on the desk in front of the screen. The little dancer blinks at me, twinkling with delight. We are old friends by now.

I can't resist it. I've always been a show-off at heart. It comes from being a handsome gray tabby. I lift a paw and pat out a few cheerful words on the screen: "Hello, Meryl! Hough are yew?"

Of course, she faints. Afterwards she doesn't seem to mind as William Richards is holding her gently and fanning her face with a sheet of manuscript paper.

"Whatever shall I do with Charlie?" she murmurs weakly.

"Teach him to spell," he says.

FLYING
FELIX

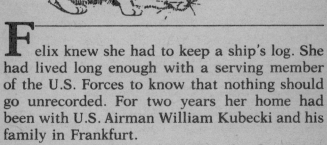

Felix knew she had to keep a ship's log. She had lived long enough with a serving member of the U.S. Forces to know that nothing should go unrecorded. For two years her home had been with U.S. Airman William Kubecki and his family in Frankfurt.

She was a dark tortoiseshell with a fine glossy coat and large bright eyes. Life was very pleasant with the Kubecki family, despite being given a masculine name. It was some name from a comic. Perhaps they spelled it Felixe. She was well fed, loved, and they played games with her.

She knew something was going to happen about a ship. "We'll have to ship Felix home," William Kubecki said a dozen times. "They'll

take care of her. We can't leave her behind.
We'll ship her out to California."

So Felix knew she had to be shipped . . . whatever that meant. She made no preparations. On
3 December they put her in a cage and locked
it. She began her log.

DAY ONE: This is a strange place. I don't like it
at all. The smell is wrong. What am I doing
here? I sniff at the sides of the cage, calling for
William, staring into the darkness. No one hears
me. There's a shattering noise and I am sliding
backwards. I am terrified. I cling frantically to
the sides, slipping and scratching . . . Where am
I going? The noise is bursting my ear drums; I
am reduced to a mass of quivering fur. Whatever
can be happening? Perhaps it's an earthquake.

I try to escape from the noise but it is
attacking me, hammering at my skull, coming
at me in great waves from everywhere. I can't
get away from it. I claw at the sides in a frenzy.
*Let me out, let me out! Janice . . . Janice . . . it's
me, your Felix.* Is this a coffin? Am I to die here?
Is this the way cats die?

I am getting used to a different, steady roaring noise now. There is food and drink in a container. Perhaps they do not want me to die after
all. The Kubeckis are a kind family; perhaps
they did not know about this shattering roar of
the ship that terrifies me.

I miss the little girl, Medine. She always plays
with me. Have they shipped her out too? Is she
in a cage, like mine? I hope she isn't. She's four

years old and rather big for a cage. She would be frightened of the noise, too.

Something is making me very sleepy. Is it something I've eaten? Perhaps if I go to sleep, I'll wake up and find this is all a nightmare.

DAY TWO: I think it's the second day. I will call it Day Two though it may still be Day One as I cannot tell how long I have slept. There is no darkness or lightness to tell me. I am not sure of the passing of time in this place. There is hope for me to escape for I have been very cunning. I have gnawed and scratched for hour after hour at the fastening of my prison. My mouth is bleeding and my claws broken to the quick.

I am feeling faintly sick. There is a strange lurching, a drifting downwards, and my ears are filling up. I am afraid they are going to burst. Suddenly the pain in my ears crucifies me as the same terrible roar splits the air, followed by a piercing scream. The ship is screaming, jolting, juddering, bouncing. I am thrown in all directions, hitting my head. The world is coming to an end. This ship has become an object of sheer terror. It is breaking up all around me.

The shuddering stops and we are moving slowly over the ground like a car. I know about cars as William takes me to the vet in his car. I hear a steel door banging and men's voices. I miaow loudly but they are making so much noise no one can hear me. They are throwing things around and moving other heavier stuff. I hope they don't throw me around.

"Careful, Joe. That one's livestock." I feel myself being lifted into the air, then put down. I miaow again.

"All right, old chap. You'll soon be in Los Angeles," someone says.

Perhaps all I have to do is wait for this Los Angeles, my thoughts in chaos, curling into a tight ball of misery in the furthest corner of the cage. *Please, William, please, Janice, please come and find me in this fiendish place.*

The door clangs shut. No one has come for me. Have they forgotten all about their Felix? I hear the low growl of this terrible noise I am coming to dread and burrow my nose into my fur and try to shut out the roar, but we are moving again and slipping and sliding. The angle is steeper than before and I am being thrown backwards, falling over and over. Something is flung open. Some time later I clamber out over the shattered bits, trembling. I am free . . .

But I am not entirely free though the new space is better than being shut in the cage. This ship place is much larger and echoing, like a dark, shaking cavern, vibrating with unseen power. It is a different prison but at least I can move about with some kind of freedom. It is full of containers and crates and boxes and piles of suitcases. The first thing is to search for food and water and a way out. But there's nothing, nothing at all. I lick a few drops of moisture off the walls. It tastes strange but it will have to do. My thirst is not too bad.

I climb high into the ceiling of my new prison, among struts and girders. There's a secure perch in the darkness where I can rest, the steady roar of the ship lulling me to sleep again.

Suddenly I am awoken by the same shrieking roar and we are bumping and jolting over the ground. I retreat further into the darkness, shrunken with fear.

A shaft of light blinds me. My pupils narrow to slits. Men are climbing through the shaft, which has widened to a large rectangle. I can see sunshine, smell the earth, the air, wide open space, and my spirits rise. The men are shouting, sweating, heaving the heavy baggage around. The big containers packed with suitcases are being trundled towards a metal lift.

"Dammit! This is broken. What the hell? It's livestock. Jeepers, what have we got loose here, buddy?"

"*Felix*, it says on the label, and *care of William Kubecki*."

"Must be a cat. A damned cat."

"Got something to catch it in? It's gotta be around here someplace."

"There's my jacket, but we oughta get a blanket or a net."

I try to judge how far I have to run to reach that square of brilliant daylight. Several men are in the way and they are searching around. I know I will never make it and the thought of being caught and put back in that cage again terrifies me. Perhaps I ought to wait for another opportunity. Perhaps the men will move out of the way.

"Not a sign of it."

"Could have slipped out when they refueled at Washington. We'd better report it. We can't spend any more time here now."

"It can't have got out. Let's have one more look."

I retreat even further into the darkness. A torch flashes perilously near. I close my eyes, knowing my eyes might reflect the light.

Their voices become distant and then the door clangs shut. What have I done? I shiver as I realize I am alone in the great cavern and trapped again. The noise begins to roar and I know this surely must be hell.

DAY THREE: It is so hot. I don't know where we are but it is like a furnace. The heat shimmers up from the ground. I crawl round the hold looking for water. (I know what it is called now for I heard men say it was a cargo hold.) I seek every drop of water off the walls. My tongue is raw from licking the rough surface.

DAY FOUR: Today I find the crusts of a sandwich, half a ham sandwich which someone has carelessly thrown away while the ship was in a building called a hangar. I munch the dried morsels in ecstasy. If only more of the engineers were like this careless man. It encourages me to seek and search but there is nothing more.

Some time later I get cramping pains in my stomach. The ham was bad.

DAY FIVE: I am stunned. This ship is a metal bird. I have seen with my own eyes from a different place that it leaves the ground and soars into the air. We fly above the clouds. I am so amazed by this new sight that for a little time I forget to be frightened. The clouds are strange stuff, white eiderdowns of cottonwool, and I wonder if I could walk on them, patting and kneading them as I used to on Janice's bed. Those halcyon days that are gone forever ...

DAY SIX: A real bird has stowed away, a stupid, frantic-eyed, fluttering thing. I contain my growing excitement and wait and watch. I am too weak to chase the creature while it is flying and squawking from perch to perch. I shall pounce when it falters.

DAY SEVEN: A whole bird—flesh, blood, bones, the lot. Though I could not cope with the feathers in my frail state. It was very surprised to see me and died instantly. Shock, no doubt. For once I feel hope. I pray for more birds to fly into the hold.

DAY EIGHT: Is this to be my life now? Am I sentenced to a nightmare existence in the sky, sometimes on the ground, my ears constantly battered by the incessant noise, the excruciating cold and those terrifying roaring times that I know now come with leaving the ground and finding the ground again. Why? Why? I know I was naughty sometimes. Once I had an accident on the floor, unable to find anyone to let me out. Another time I stole some cheese in the kitchen and dragged it under a chair to eat. And I broke a bowl as I jumped on to a cluttered surface. All sins, they told me. Naughty pussy, they scolded in cross voices. *Forgive me. Take me out of this hell hole.*

DAY NINE: I am tormented by thirst.

DAY ELEVEN: I am losing count of the days. Where are we now? I am ravaged by hunger and thirst. I no longer wonder what is happening and why. Time has collapsed into a meaningless pattern of noise and roars and shrieks. Sometimes I sleep through the endless droning, trying to find some warmth in the relentless cold. My fur is no longer thick. There are quiet times when we are in the empty hold called a hangar and then the stillness is beyond the grave.

DAY TWELVE: I have eaten some flies and crunched them with relish. They swarmed in when we stopped at a hot, dry place. The air was full of spicy smells, fragrant scent of blossoms that blew in, pale petals on a hot wind . . . and the flies. I would not have touched a fly once, whisked the pesky thing off my nose. Now I am not so choosy. Life is reduced to flies and water. No trees, no leaves, no soft laps, no beds, no chairs, no words of kindness, no love. Nothing.

DAY THIRTEEN OR FOURTEEN: The humidity is stifling. Hot, sultry air envelops the hold in a heavy wetness. What is this place where the air is drenched with moisture? But it is good for me in one way; the droplets run down the walls into pools and I lap the acidic water gratefully.

DAY SIXTEEN: Sometimes I can hear the sea. My ears are constantly bombarded by noise but, despite that, my hearing is still acute. The sea is not far away. Oh, the smells of the sea bring back such memories. They are enticing smells of food, of fish. There is a package in the hold that is soaked with this smell and I tear at the wet wrapping, eating the paper, but I cannot get to the inside and nearly die with disappointment.

DAY NINETEEN: These dark-skinned loaders are also careless with food. I find a few bits of flat dough, baked dry, some with a scrape of soft tomato or meat sauce still clinging to it. I will eat anything and be thankful.

DAY TWENTY: I cannot endure much more of this misery.

DAY WHAT: I do not know what . . .

DAY TWENTY-SEVEN: They have seen me! I was unthinking, dozing, sunken into a weary stupor. A man is shouting and his voice is threatening.

"It's a rat, a damned great rat! Get a stick." A light flashes across me.

"What a size!"

"That's not a rat. It's a cat. Blimey, it looks half starved."

"You'd be starving in here, Buster."

"Let's try and catch it. Puss, puss . . ."

I race away on wobbly legs. I know every inch of the hold now. I know places so small that a man could not even get his hand into them. I am so thin, I can squeeze myself into these smallest of places.

There is so much commotion going on, I hardly know what is happening beyond the wild thudding of my heart.

"We'll have to coax it out," comes a woman's voice. I stop in my tracks. It is so long since I have heard a woman's voice that for a moment I think it is Janice. Then I realize that the voice has a different tone and accent. "It's frightened, of course. Perhaps if I go on with the plane to Frankfurt, it'll come to me of its own accord. It must be starving. I'll get some food."

"Make sure you're back in time for New Year, Jane."

The woman called Jane is traveling in the cargo hold with me. I eye her warily from my high perch. She puts out food but I do not move. She wanders about, trying to find me, but she doesn't know where I am in the ceiling. It is a honeycomb of metal struts and I am very small. I lick a few drops of moisture and watch her closely.

DAY TWENTY-EIGHT: We are flying on to Washington, the woman called Jane says. She was cold in the hold, too, but she had warm clothes and rugs, and I would have loved to curl up near her. She is leaving me to go back to her work.

DAY TWENTY-NINE: Frankfurt again and soon we will be back at somewhere called Heathrow. I don't know where anywhere is any more ... I am sleeping more and more ... soon I will not wake up ... it is only a matter of time. I shall not really mind.

"Got it! Got it!" One of the loading staff unceremoniously grabbed the cat by the scruff of its neck and hauled it down into daylight. It was just a bedraggled bundle of fur, terrified and starving, its sore, encrusted eyes wide with fear.

"Hold it firmly but gently. We don't want to lose it again," said Jane, thankful that they had got the cat out of the hold at last, even if it was New Year's Day. She wrapped the pathetic trembling creature in a cardigan and hurried across the tarmac to her office. Jane Ford was the Pan Am loading supervisor; she also loved cats. She had three of her own at home.

"Let's get some milk down it before it dies on us. And call a vet, please. It'll probably have to go into quarantine."

The emaciated cat was wary of the saucer of milk in case it was a trap. It moved cautiously on thin and shaky legs. It seemed to have forgotten how to lap; then suddenly the smell was too enticing. The cat fell upon the milk, almost dizzy with excitement, a trembling purr threatening to drown her as she gulped down the milk in panic-stricken swallows.

Some hours later, after being examined by a vet, a bewildered Felix was being cared for in North London and fed carefully monitored small amounts of milky food. She was in a small room but there was no noise beyond quiet voices and gentle hands. The lack of noise was velvet to her bruised ears. Perhaps she had gone deaf. She slept the first dreamless sleep for a long time.

Jane and the Pan Am staff collected money to pay for the cat's quarantine. In the meantime, staff at Pan Am's New York office finally traced the cat's owners—the Kubeckis, now living in California. They were overjoyed that their pet had been found.

On 21 January, Felix flew home to her family as a VIP in the first-class cabin of Flight PA 121, a new collar and bell around her neck, just in case she escaped again. She flew in the lap of luxury with champagne and caviar, her fare paid by Pan Am. Felix preferred Jane's lap, posing for newspaper photographs with her paws round Jane's neck.

Felix turned up her nose at the caviar; the tuna fish was more to her liking.

"No stowing away this time, Felix," said Jane, feeling the soft body go rigid as the plane's engines began to warm up. "And don't be frightened."

She stroked the proud head to calm the cat's fears. The tenseness began to leave the small frame as Jane's fingers conveyed a message of comfort. "You're going home in style."

Felix had flown approximately 179,000 miles in the pressurized cargo hold of *Belle of the Skies*, a Boeing 747, the equivalent of seven times round the world.

She endured more than sixty takeoffs and landings. Among the places she visited were Los Angeles, Washington, San Francisco, Miami, Nassau in the Bahamas, the Leeward Islands, Rio de Janeiro, Sao Paulo, Buenos Aires, Santiago, Guayaquil in Ecuador, Rome, Zurich, Geneva, Paris, Riyadh and Delhi.

SEXY
REXY

T he trouble with Pixie was that he didn't feel sexy, so he didn't want to. He knew how, of course. Mating was a natural function for animals even if fraught with inhibitions for humans.

But Pixie was different. Every time a little queen was introduced to the household, he regarded her as a special visitor, gave her his favorite toys and treated her like porcelain.

The three sisters had found Pixie wandering along a high-hedged Devon lane, one hot sunny afternoon when a heat haze rose from the sea like steam. The cat was walking aimlessly, shimmering like a mirage, sprayed with pollen from the nodding wild hollyhocks. He was the most unusual cat they had ever come across. They were quite astounded.

"Just look at that coat. Remarkable," said Doreen, the breeder, eyes squinting keenly. "I've never seen anything quite like it. It's truly sensational."

"Extraordinary genetic make-up," said Maureen, the geneticist. "A really interesting mutation."

"What a darling little pixie face," said Coreen, the cat-lover and by far the youngest of the three sisters. She went down on her knees and held out a slim hand. "What a sweet, gentle expression."

The cat sat in the lane and stared at the sisters with worldly-wise eyes. He saw them as big, middle-sized and small. The small-sized one was cooing at him. His self-possessed attitude stated clearly that he could take care of himself, thank you, but would tolerate a degree of human companionship if really necessary.

"Do you think it's a stray?" said Coreen hopefully. "There's not a house for miles around."

"It's certainly not a feral," said Doreen. "No feral would sit that still. It would have been off like a shot."

"I'd give anything to study its chromosomes, how the carrying of X or Y determines the curly coat, the color, the sex," said Maureen. "It's a Cornish Rex, of course."

"But this is Devon," said Coreen.

"I've read about them but never seen one before," Doreen mused as she walked round him. He shook a petal off his forehead.

"Someone has given this puss a perm," Coreen smiled, wanting to run her fingers through the tight waves.

Her sisters turned on her with exasperation. They did not have twenty-four-hour patience. "You don't listen, Coreen. They are supposed to look like that. Their coats are naturally curly."

The Rex cat followed them at a distance for the entire length of their walk. They discussed his curly coat, the beautiful modulating waves of closely lying fur. They were amused by his curly whiskers and eyebrows. The hind legs were taller than the front, giving him a rather curious, elegant gait. His head was a medium wedge, ears large and pointed. His eyes were large, almond-shaped, green chartreuse in color.

"A truly curious cat," they sighed longingly.

"Are we going to keep him?" asked Coreen.

They hesitated. "We'd have to advertise, make all the proper enquiries. A Rex cat doesn't just go wandering."

"But he seems to want to come with us. I shall call him Pixie," said Coreen, deciding.

Her sisters groaned in unison. "It's a male, Coreen. You can't call him Pixie."

"Aren't there any male pixies?" she argued.

"At least she hasn't suggested Big Ears," Maureen murmured in an aside.

"If we are going to breed from him, we shall have to find him a proper, registered name," Doreen added.

"Devona Lanium Rexus," said Maureen, who had once studied Latin. "Found in a Devon lane. What could be more appropriate?"

The three sisters, who were well known around

the area for being eccentric, put "Found in a Devon Lane" advertisements in all the local papers, stuck posters on telegraph poles, cards in shop windows. They left no line of enquiry unexplored. There was even a mention on local radio. This last inspired avenue had a momentous result. An anonymous woman phoned in saying she didn't want the cat any more because it was funny-looking.

"Funny-looking!" said Coreen indignantly, her arms full of cat as she stood in the garden, gazing at the endless, stretching sky. "How callous. He's beautiful."

After this public statement of rejection, the sisters felt free to take the animal into their home, though he had already installed himself with little fuss or trouble.

"Er . . . Pixie," said Doreen, who could never quite bring herself to say his name, "is a Chinchilla Rex. I've been reading a book on Rex colors. 'White undercoat; coat on back, flanks, head and tail sufficiently tipped with black to give known sparkling appearance," she quoted.

"My sparkling Pixie," crooned Coreen, cradling him.

" 'Rim of eyes, lips and nose outlined in black,' " Doreen went on.

Maureen brought through a tray of tea, cream and jam and scones. "He's good enough to breed from. We ought to get him a queen."

"We'll get you a queen, little prince," Coreen whispered to him, child-like and secretive, her fine hair falling all over his face.

"It's a bit risky, isn't it?" said Doreen, taking

two scones and piling on the cream. "Do you understand properly about the chromosomes? We could end up with a whole litter of short-haired moggies."

"How lovely," said Coreen, clapping her hands. "We could keep them all."

The more the elder sisters delved into the subject, the more complicated it became. Careful selection was needed to re-create the beautiful coats because Devon Rex had an h factor which could produce hairless cats, and early inter-crossing of genes might produce normal coats. Their daily conversation was devoted to genes and crossings and standard points.

Coreen did not bother to listen. She played with Pixie, sang him little songs, told him her favorite fairy stories, took him for walks among the hedgerows.

None of them knew that Pixie would decide it all for them. He was quietly intelligent. He had his own box of toys and special playthings. He put them away in the same place every night so that he knew where to find them in the morning. He slept at the foot of Coreen's bed, waking her early with a series of gentle pats on the face, peering closely at her fluttering lashes. He was unaware that his role in life was being determined for him. He could not tell them he was no Romeo, no stud, no sire.

The queen arrived by train, in an escape-proof carrier. She was calling loudly. The sisters introduced the elegant blue-point Siamese. They had been advised to go for Pixie's unusual pixie face and deeply waved coat. The mating could result in a prestigious Blue Rex.

"This is Miss Misty Silver," they told Pixie, putting the noisy queen on the floor. "She's come all the way from Plymouth in the train to see you. Isn't that nice?"

The exotic Siamese was shouting and barking incessantly. She curled up on the floor, one paw over her face, giving Pixie the eye. Pixie retreated, appalled by the noise. He searched in his toy box for an orange ball dimpled with tiny holes. He hooked it out delicately and sent it scudding across the floor to the Siamese.

She looked at it with horror and astonishment and raced up the curtains. Pixie patted the ball from paw to paw like a juggler; he rolled over, still juggling, and scored an own goal with a deft putt under a chair. Miss Misty Silver clawed along the floral pelmet, howling. She hadn't come all this way on a dirty train just to play ball.

The Siamese went home three days later, somewhat subdued, not in kitten, but with a nifty new line in ball games.

The second queen learned how to fight a brown paper bag and the rudiments of shadow boxing; the third queen exhausted herself playing hide-and-seek with Pixie all over the house. The floorboards echoed with scampering feet and pounces of discovery. Each evening they curled down companionably together, good friends, but with nothing more pressing on their minds than the invention of new and more amazing places to hide. When it was time for the queen to go home, she had to be forcibly removed from the upstairs linen basket.

Pixie was taken to the vet for a check-up. He thought it a totally unnecessary intrusion, resented the intimacy and withdrew into eloquent silence with an expression of hurt and indignation.

"Your Rex is one hundred per cent cat," said the new vet, a studious young man called Andrew. "He's a friendly cat, not an amorous cat. Don't push him. Enjoy his unique companionship. Does it matter if he sires kittens or not?"

The breeder and geneticist sisters both looked disappointed but Coreen gathered the wavy-coated cat up into her arms.

"I don't care whether he does or does not," she said. "It's not important to me."

"Let Nature take its course," said the vet, washing his hands and thinking how charming the youngest sister looked with the unusual cat in her amns, her pale frizzy hair tumbling about her shoulders. "He may give you a surprise one day."

Eventually Doreen and Maureen reluctantly had to give up their ambition to produce a Rex cat of distinction to show. It was costing a fortune in returned fees, and all Pixie wanted to do was to play games with his visitors. They studied the subject, had heated discussions and read every word published. They longed to learn somewhere of a miracle food supplement or a fail-safe aphrodisiac for felines.

"It might be something terribly simple like

strawberries," said Doreen optimistically, watching a magpie in half-mourning puncturing their lawn with his sharp beak. "Or shellfish. We could try giving him shellfish."

"I'm going through those gene tables again. Perhaps I missed something really important," said Maureen.

"Perhaps Pixie is like a human and he has to be in love," said Coreen, quite seriously for once. She thought about being in love and wondered what it was like. She knew she loved Pixie to the point of distraction and that she worried terribly if she did not know where he was. It must be something like that.

Some months later, Andrew called round, controlled excitement in his voice. "My Cornish Rex queen has just produced a litter of two Red Rex kittens with brilliant copper eyes and one long-haired Rex kitten with green chartreuse eyes. I don't know the father but I can make a calculated guess. Do you want one of the kittens?"

"We'll have all three," said Doreen and Maureen in unison, ambition bursting afresh in their ample bosoms.

"Have they got Pixie faces?" Coreen wanted to know.

"Oh yes," said Andrew. "Definitely pixie faces."

"Then Pixie fell in love at last," she said with a pleased sigh. "He only needed to fall in love."

"Sometimes it takes a long time," said the young vet hesitantly. "Finding the right person and all that."

"I know," said Coreen. "Meanwhile you have

to keep playing ball." She could see her sisters looking at her, their faces momentarily clouded. For years they had taken care of her, protected her from the harshness of life. She knew she was different, that in many spheres she had never grown up and never would. But there were a hundred meanings of happiness. She would find her own special haven.

The young vet was anxious to leave. He had a lot of calls to make and, being shy, he'd had to steel himself to face the three formidable sisters. But he had one more thing to say. "When would you like to come and see the kittens?" he asked, speaking to Coreen directly.

"I'll come today," she said, making the first adult decision of her life and knowing it was a good one.

LITTLE GOOSE

He thought it was a rat, but he was wrong. It was wild mink, a sleek wet creature that slithered through the undergrowth with a speed that had the hungry cat panting.

The cat had not eaten for days. He had traveled a long way, picking up a few mice here and there, the odd burger bun. Hardly enough to keep the thread of life together. Traveling rough did not suit him. He was soft, used to a more leisurely and comfortable life with a kindly woman who cared for him and spoilt him like a precious child. She was old, but Thomas had not known that old was fraught with danger and that his contented existence could be shattered by a fishy word like salmonella.

She was taken off in an ambulance, barely

conscious, her face pale with sweat. Thomas watched from a fence, not understanding. It was fortunate in a way that he was locked out of the house and not locked in. He would definitely have died if she had collapsed before letting him out for his nightly run. It was the last thing she did before calling a neighbor for help.

Thomas waited for several days for the woman to come back. But she never returned. Hunger drove him to the woods and outhouses of nearby farms. He needed quite a bit of practice before he caught anything. Starvation was a stern teacher and finally he caught an ancient dormouse that was tough and juiceless but nevertheless edible.

Thomas moved in an ever widening circle from his home, taking in fields and paths and high hedgerows, beginning to know the layout of the surrounding countryside as well as he had once known his own little back garden.

Chasing the mink came at the end of a long fruitless night. The sleek creature had not seen Thomas curled up in the hedge, thin and battle-scarred, one ear ragged and bloodied from a fight with a half-mad feral staked out in a farm barn.

The mink slithered out of a reed bed, dark coat wet and gleaming. Thomas still thought it was a rat and pounced. The mink was too fast and too clever. He ran with Thomas in desperate pursuit, over fields, through swathes of reeds, screens and ditches, under a gap in a mesh fence, into an alien place which Thomas had never seen before.

The cat paused fractionally, nose twitching, alerted by a new pungent smell. In that split second, the mink escaped.

Suddenly out of the early-morning mist a huge white apparition reared up at him like an avenging angel, long neck swaying in reptilian parody. It was an awesome creature, wings slapping the air with a fast explosive noise. Its flat black feet stamped the ground angrily, dust flying into Thomas's eyes.The black beak gaped, emitting a ferocious cackle as beady eyes focused on him with evil intent.

Thomas was transfixed with terror. In all his life he had never seen such a monster. Nor would he see another, for these were surely his last moments on earth. He thought of his sweet life with the woman, of her gentle hands, of the warmth of her love and care. And for it all to end like this, crunched and mangled to a horrible nothingness by that razor-sharp beak. It did not seem fair. But if he had to die, then die he would. To die at the mercy of such a monster would be no humble death.

The white wings brushed across his face and the beak clipped his sore ear. The pain made Thomas yelp and leap high into the air, much to the monster's surprise. The long white neck swerved and wavered, then reared backwards, ready to lunge into a new attack.

Thomas landed in something wet. He slid down a slippery bank and found himself floundering in shallow water. The white creature peered down at him, puzzlement fractionally replacing the fierceness in its eyes. The cat tried to scramble out, bedraggled and wretched, gray fur flattened, body and neck scrawny.

Three grey cygnets swam over, circling with a delicate paddle, friendly and curious. Two of the cygnets belonged to the pen who had attacked Thomas; the third had been added to the rearing pen for her to foster.

As Thomas floundered in the muddy water, the pen began to wonder if this odd creature had been added to her young and she was expected to look after it. Her cygnets were coming to no harm as the cat struggled to find a foothold. It certainly couldn't swim.

The cob looked on with suspicion, waving his neck, flapping his wings in protest at this disturbance to his family. But, as his pen seemed less perturbed now, he quietened down and waited.

They were waiting for the clank and squeak of the wooden cart being trundled along the path from the sanctuary stores to bring their daily rations of eel grass and wild watercress. These edibles grew on the bed of the lagoon but the purpose of the rearing enclosures was to enable the sanctuary to release stronger young who were able to withstand the rigors of winter.

Thomas lay trembling against the bank of the enclosure, rear legs trailing in the water, his front claws clamped on to some reed stubble. He was amazed he was still alive. In an unconnected part of his mind, he registered a growing noise. It was unlike anything he had ever heard before: a volume of clacking and shrieks as if a pack of devils was approaching.

A white swarm appeared in the distance like a cloud, gliding over the lagoon, growing ever larger. Thomas saw it rise out of the water, a great flapping, clattering wave of wings and necks and feathers, heads bobbing and weaving, hundreds of pigeon-toed flat feet slapping the ground. Wriggle-wraggle, wiggle-woggle, the herd plodded determinedly towards him. This was a hell beyond all imagination.

The noise of the rusty cart wheels was lost in the deafening clamor as the din rose in the air, taking on fearsome shapes that flashed across his vision. Suddenly a swatch of wet, slippery grass landed on Thomas's head, followed almost immediately by handfuls of watercress. The cygnets swam eagerly towards their breakfast with sweet baby noises, daintily pecking the grass off Thomas, never nipping or biting him. He kept very still.

They were surprised that he did not eat the green stuff. The pen swam over to look at her reluctant fourth baby but could not make out what was the matter. She nibbled at some grass floating on the water, hoping he would follow her example.

Meanwhile the herd fed at the water's edge, a writhing mass of white heads and bobbing beaks, the grass and cress falling on them like confetti.

After they had eaten, the cob and pen began their rubber-necked grooming, twisting and elongating their necks into pecking contortions. Thomas was mesmerized by their performance. He could reach parts found impossible by other four-footed animals, but truly the swans were capable of amazing dexterity. It was while he was watching them that something silvery-gray darted past him.

All his reflexes were automatic. He pounced, scooped the small fish out of the water and swallowed it in one satisfied gulp. It was only a stickleback, but to a starving cat it was a morsel from heaven. Perhaps, after all, this was not the end of his life. Slowly be pulled himself out of the rearing enclosure and explored the immediate area. The pond was connected to the large lagoon by a small channel along which water flowed. The fish, disturbed by the chaos of feeding time, were fleeing up the channel. His paw flashed out and caught another, then another. It was so easy.

He began to think more rationally. The saltwater lagoon must be teeming with fish. He could live here forever. There were mullet, bass, eels . . . fish far too big for his present fishing skills. Soon the sea-birds were showing him how to fish. Little terns hovered over the water, plunging into the wavelets to scoop up mullet fry and smelt. Thomas had to content himself with fishing from the slippery edge but he became clever at balancing and timing the pounce of his sharp claws.

At nightfall, he fell asleep, curled up in a nearby nest of old reeds and dried grass, his stomach satisfied. The pen closed her eyes and tucked her head under a wing, relieved that her odd new baby was becoming part of the family and the imprinting was beginning. Soon he might learn to recognize his parents' calls. It all took time.

Thomas did not wander far from the safety of the rearing enclosure for several days. The pen protected him from other swans and reared up, wings flapping, if any approached too curiously. The cygnets accepted him as one of them, innocently amused by his attempts at swimming. Thomas began to trust the pen in a strange way, though he was wary of the cob.

As his confidence increased, so he began to explore the sanctuary but keeping well away from the great herd of swans that rose from the lagoon with regularity every mealtime.

"Little goose," said one of the men, spotting him among the reeds. "What do you think you are? A swan?"

"Perhaps he thinks he's going to turn into one, like the ugly duckling," chuckled another man.

There were a lot of birds in the reed bed—warblers, wrens, moorhens, coots—but Thomas had the sense to leave them alone. This was a sanctuary for all and only the lagoon was his pantry.

He discovered it had fluid fences; be could leave any time. The acres of reed and water were a song without words and the daily theater never bored him. He could always watch the sea, his mind absorbing the mystery of the tide, the magic of its endless waves.

But Thomas was quite surprised when people arrived in a steady trickle, families with children in pushchairs, the elderly in wheelchairs.

The swans mistook every creaking wheel for the food trolley and rose like a vacillating wraith from the lagoon, scaring the visitors, and lording at the cameras' clicking.

Thomas got used to the visitors, peering hopefully to see if the woman was among them. She never was. Sometimes a child dropped an ice-cream or a biscuit, and he was on the spot in a second, his long tongue savoring the change in diet.

There were dormice and harvest mice in the woods near the reed bed but Thomas was now too well fed to give them more than a passing fright. He saw a rabbit in the moonlight, sitting up and twitching his whiskers, but left him in peace.

Thomas became as at home in the water as on land though he preferred to keep his fur dry. Instinctively he realized that his acceptance and protection by the cob and pen depended to some extent on his resemblance to their cygnets. They had accepted him as the herd had accepted the solitary Rosy Caribbean Flamingo that flew among them one cold day in 1981 and was still there, stalking the lagoon in lonely splendor on matchstick legs.

A small child caught sight of Thomas sunning himself among the reeds. She waggled pudgy fingers at him and tugged at her mother's skirt.

"Look, a pussy cat," she said.

"No, dear, they're swans. This is a swannery."

"Cat," said the child, stubbornly.

"Swan," said the mother.

Thomas stretched out in the sun and flicked

away an insect with his tail. They could call him anything. His mind drifted away into an extended dream from the past. He dreamed he was chasing a rat and pounced, but he was wrong. It was a mink, a sleek wet creature that slithered through the undergrowth with a speed that had the hungry cat panting. The cat had not eaten for days ... He had traveled a long way, picking up ... a few mice ... here ... and there ...

SAM, SAM . . .

This is a strange story to relate and you may not believe it, or want to believe it. You may not even understand the implications. If not, then it is simply an epitaph to Sam and all the other Sams that have been here.

There is no way to describe the grief of losing a beloved cat. Even now tears come into my eyes when I think of those many dear feline friends who have died over the years. They never quite leave me, something of each always remains, some memory of delight reminding me of their enchanting ways. My cats have always been loving and beloved, so perhaps it is the aura of their love that still lingers.

One guilty thought always comes unbidden into this grief. It is the prospect that at some time, but not too soon, a new kitten or kittens will take that empty place in my family of cats and the whole process of loving and losing will begin again.

Sometimes, on bad days, I am consumed with pre-grief. This is a wasteful and useless emotion. I cradle my lion-cat, a great bundle of long pale ginger fur, and cannot bear the thought that one day he will go and his lovely coat rot. I am besotted by his handsomeness, his outrageous personality, his macho image. Everything he does is full of power and grace; there is not an inelegant movement in his body.

I mourn in this early way over my old tortie Colorpoint too, shabbily beautiful like a fading aristocrat, knowing she is nearing the end of her days. She is fourteen years old, silly and senile, and we allow her to be endearingly eccentric.

My Somali was another extravagantly beautiful creature; hardly of this world at times and yet with such an abundant personality that often I caught an intention on his face as if he were about to speak. Words would not have surprised me at all. Sometimes I heard echoes of words as if he had spoken straight into my mind.

The crowning glory of my Somali was his soft and silky coat, so smooth and fine, his adult ruff the perfect frame for a sweet and gentle face. He was an apricot-ticked-black; each hair was banded many times with black and apricot, starting with black at the tip. It gave him a lovely, sparkly effect, as if his coat was shot with light. And I loved the rim of pale fur that looked like spectacles around his eyes and gave him an innocent, wide-eyed expression when in reality he was as street-wise as any urchin moggie.

His name was Sam behind closed doors, though, of course, his registered names were an exotic concoction of nonsense and elitism.

"Sam, Sam . . ." I often sang to him, "do you know where I am? I am here . . . waiting for you."

And he would run like the wind, coming from out of nowhere, to twist himself round my ankles.

Sam showed an immense and lively curiosity about everything. If I was reading the newspaper, then he had to read it too. When I brought home the shopping, every item had to be inspected. If I was working at my typewriter, he sat solidly on the pile of typescript, watching the flicking of my fingers with a concentration guaranteed to produce a crop of errors.

Make-up time in the bathroom was also high on entertainment value. Sam sat in the wash basin, absorbed in every move, regarding with tolerance my efforts to paint out the years. Then he would stretch up on his hind legs and plant his paws on my shoulders and give my chin a consolatory nudge.

"Well tried, old girl," he might have been saying.

The years with Sam were rich. He made them so. He paid his rent money a thousandfold. I don't believe that cats hate being laughed at. He always seemed to join in, perhaps pretending to be offended, but actually grinning away with a smug expression when a joke had worked on us.

There cannot be any truth in the rumor that cats have a restricted intelligence or lack of brain power. I would like to have tested Sam's IQ. He certainly had a brain and a wicked intelligence.

He also had his own inner clock. He appeared like magic at meal times, to the minute. He could hear the refrigerator door opening from the end of the garden. He recognized different cupboard sounds and knew the corner one where the Munchies were kept. He observed when I was getting ready to go to work, and put-out time became hide-under-the-bed time.

He knew when I needed comforting, when a lapful of cats was worth its weight in gold. He saw when I was ill and asked for nothing, nothing at all, simply curling up on my bed at the back of my knees, as quiet as a whisper, only that soft breathing telling me I was not alone. I think he would have starved rather than leave me.

Sometimes when he was bored, he played at getting under my feet. It was a deliberate ploy like a football player dribbling a ball towards the goalposts. Rather than tripping over his tail and breaking an ankle, I would pick him up and fuss and cuddle him, which was just what he wanted.

Sociability was Sam's middle name. He practically showed visitors round the house, introduced them to the best chair, inspected their shoes, skirts, trouser hems. Handbags were a favorite. My friends learned to keep their hand-bags closed or he would have half the contents out on the floor, grading them from zero to maximum playworthiness.

My friends also learned not to ignore him but to say hello politely and ask after his health. Bad manners got the full treatment of infantile pestering. He knew exactly how to irritate an indifferent visitor.

And how could he distinguish my footsteps on the pavement from a whole cavalcade of feet that walked home from the station each evening? But he only came to the gate for my footsteps. I often saw his light form streaking across the garden to be the first at the gate to greet me, while the other cats were still uncurling themselves from various outposts. How could he tell it was me?

I don't want to talk about his heart attack.

The house felt all wrong, empty. The other cats were subdued, going about the days soft-pawed and undemanding. They ate out of habit, came to me with gentle affection and comfort. They knew he had gone, for I could not just let him disappear, not after all those years of living together.

So I had showed them Sam in his eternal sleep. Strange how cats can dismiss death. One sniff and they turned away.

It was quite a long time before I realized that Sam was still with me. I suppose I had become unseeing and unhearing. I was working at my typewriter one day when I became very aware that I was being watched. My fingers fumbled on the keys. I looked around carefully in case one of my other cats was about to surprise me, but they were all out.

"Sam, Sam . . ." I sang softly. "Do you know where I am?"

There was no sound in the room, only my breathing. Everything was very still. Then I heard the faintest rustle of paper, as if something was stirring. Yet I saw nothing.

I went into the kitchen to make some coffee, feeling a little unnerved, and I tripped over something. Holding on to the counter edge, I looked down. I had tripped over empty air.

As I opened the refrigerator door for milk, a chilly breeze brushed my ankles like the touch of fur.

The coffee cooled as I sat and thought about the past few days. I remembered odd fleeting sensations that were difficult to pin down, but there remained a strong lingering feeling of not being alone.

Some time afterwards I was ill with influenza and though, strangely, the cats had taken a unanimous vote and all decided to keep me company in bed, there was one more. I could feel a shape against the back of my knees, just the slightest weight.

The other cats were in a sprawling heap at the foot of the bed, intertwined, using each other as pillows. But I could definitely feel this weight against my leg. I put my hand down hopefully, my eyes closed . . . but there was nothing. Perhaps it was the fever and the pounding headache.

I dreamed that night that I was walking with Sam and he was as tall as a man, and he walked upright like a man, with my hand clasped in his paw. He took me to a high hill with a panoramic view of the whole world. Rivers and plains, mountains and oceans flowed continuously in all directions. He turned to me, his gentle face full of love, and in my dream, he could speak words.

"I know where you are," he said.

When I awoke, I was immensely comforted. I wrote my dream in my diary before I could forget it. I seemed to come out of my grief, and when I had recovered my health, I took up my usual busy life with all the fun and dramas of a cat family.

I don't normally read the free paper that comes through the letterbox. There really isn't time for any more reading and it's mostly adverts anyway. I was putting the paper on the wastepaper pile for collection, when a photograph on the front page caught my eye. It was the face of a tiny kitten. The caption said that the six-week-old kitten had been found injured and was being cared for at a rescue center, but that no owner had come forward and if it was not claimed then it would have to be put down.

I was on the telephone immediately.

"No," I said. "It's not my kitten, but yes, I will have it if no one claims it. No, I don't mind if it's got a broken leg. What's a broken leg? You don't put down people if they break a leg."

Four weeks later Peg-leg was fit enough to come home to us. He was a moggie of uncertain breed with gray and black splodges and a rather squashed-in face. He was not particularly attractive with these indistinguishable marks, but he had a lively, independent personality and soon made himself at home. His slight limp was no disability at all when it came to the rough-and-tumble of community life. In fact, he threw himself into the fray with all the courage and vitality of a young male.

It was when he began to do certain things that my heart stood still. He sat squarely on my newspaper when I was trying to read it; he inspected my shopping with time-consuming thoroughness; he was fascinated by my typing, walking all over the desk as if it were his personal playground.

One morning I was in the bathroom, beginning the daily refit of my face, when I felt rather than heard a cat leap up beside me. It was Peg-leg. He sat quietly, short gray tail curled tidily over his toes, watching me with my pots of paints and brushes. Then when I had finished, he stretched up and put his paws on each of my shoulders and nudged my chin. His almond-shaped eyes were glinting with amusement. It was then I noticed a clearly defined white rim of fur round his eyes like spectacle frames ...

I was shaken. I went to my diary and looked up the date of my dream: 26 February 1990. I worked out Peg-leg's probable birthday from the date of the newspaper and my telephone call. It all seemed to fit. Peg-leg was born the last week in February. It could have been the same date.

The knowledge hung in my mind all day, that unknowing, tantalizing wondering. When I walked home from the station that evening, Peg-leg was the first to the gate, gray fur rippling.

After I had greeted and stroked all the cats in their turn—my lovely lion-cat, the fearless black Persian hunter, the dainty tortoiseshell, our elderly Colorpoint stumbling forward on arthritic legs—I turned back to Peg-leg. I took him down to the far end of the garden, where we could be alone. He loved being carried and was purring and nudging me and pushing his claws into my hair. I put him down on the grass and walked away quite some distance, not looking back. I was trembling with apprehension, my hands clasped tightly.

"Sam, Sam . . ." I sang, "do you know where I am? I am here . . . waiting for you."

And he ran like the wind, on cue, coming from out of nowhere, to twist himself round my ankles.

KIPPERBANG'S PET

Nearly everybody had a pet. Kipper knew that. He was fairly sure of his facts. He was always hearing people say things like: "How's your pet dog?" "What a little pet." "That's my pet hate!"

And most people enjoyed having a pet. They fed it, bought it presents, played with it. They were pleasant companions, constant, loyal, durable, though not exactly durable in the forever sense. There was the "I'm never going to have another pet" type remark—"it's too upsetting when they go."

It seemed the majority of people got over being upset and eventually another pet appeared in the household, be it dog/cat/mongoose/boa constrictor or daft, twittering bird.

Kipper longed to have a pet of his own. He saw nothing funny in it. It was not as funny as his name. People fell about with hysterics when they heard his full name.

"T'yang, yang, kipperbang? Surely you don't stand at the door calling T'yang yang kipperbang? It's a ridiculous name for a cat."

"I know it's a ridiculous name," said Jo, his owner. "But he's just so . . . beautiful. There just isn't a name in existence that's beautiful enough for him."

There was no logic in that, concluded Kipper. At least in the interest of expediency, his name was usually shortened to Kipper. Even the abbreviation caused untold hilarity. It was not fair. He was sure he did not look like a fish.

"Of course he doesn't look like a fish," said Jo, brushing his long tortoiseshell fur. He had deeply intelligent amber eyes, a white nose and long white whiskers. All this and a gentle, affectionate nature. It was this sweet nature that made him yearn for a pet of his own.

He loved Jo and always would, but that was a different emotion. For a start she was a towering black-haired giant, and giants were unpredictable. A pet was usually smaller, though there was probably some fruit-cake with an elephant or a dinosaur for a pet.

He wanted something very small and lovable. Something he could look after and cherish and protect. He began to keep his eyes open for a pet. Somewhere out there was a pet longing to belong to him.

Kipper thought he had found the ideal quiet

domesticated pet one balmy summer afternoon. It was decorative with fine veining on a smooth, glossy surface, but underneath it was rough and gritty . . . an interesting contrast of texture. He curled his tail round it, surveying the world with pride. He had his own pet at last.

For several days he barely left his pet's side. Only quick snacks and calls of nature took priority. After a week he had to admit to a slight growing disappointment. His pet's play-potential was practically nil. Occasionally it rolled down the path, which could only be classed as mildly exciting. It ate nothing despite Kipper's offerings of dead mice, potato peelings and squashed spiders.

It slept most of the time; in fact it slept all of the time.

"Kipper has got a touch of the sun," said Jo. "He's been sitting on a pebble all week."

One day Kipper's pebble got swept up and thrown away. Kipper was slightly upset. Being swept up was not the same as going to the vet's or being put to sleep. It had an ethereal quality as if his pet was floating through space, homing in on some planetary ancestor.

Kipper's second pet was an immediate hit. It moved and it ate, and that attracted Kipper from the start. It had already half digested a stale cheeseburger but still managed to take off on an unmanned flight. Kipper chased it round the garden, patted it into the air, tossed it into flower beds. It was all tremendous fun. Kipper danced sideways, boxing and shadowing. It was the ideal pet, never complaining, never tiring, always game for another game.

But one morning disaster hit Kipper's new pet. It was a lethal combination of heavy rain and Jo's bicycle. The front tyre flattened the pet beyond all recognition. It lay sadly in a sodden mass.

"Fast-food bags everywhere," said Jo, scooping it up into the dustbin. "People are so untidy."

Kipper sat dejectedly under a lilac tree, inhaling the heady perfume to calm his confused emotions. He had really liked his bag-pet, much better than his pebble-pet. He was going through pets at an alarming rate. Soon there wouldn't be any left for him. He stretched elegantly but aimlessly and wandered round the garden, sniffing back a little sadness.

He lay out on a sun-warmed patch of newly mown grass and yawned pinkly. He'd got absolutely nothing to do now that he didn't have a pet. He dozed off in the sunshine, toes twitching, chasing butterflies and moths in his dreams.

The merest sound woke him. The tiniest creature was not two inches from his nose. It was the prettiest rosy-red, shiny and smooth, with dainty spots in a pattern and little gauzy things whirring in the air.

Kipper was instantly besotted. He gazed, transfixed, till his eyes crossed, hardly daring to breathe in case the great rough sounds frightened the tiny creature. It was clinging perilously to a hewn stalk of grass. When Kipper thought of how close to extermination from that monstrous mowing machine it had been, he went cold with horror.

It was the pet of his dreams. It did not seem in the least frightened of him. It slithered down the stalk, then on fragile, wobbly legs moved closer to Kipper. It climbed up the fur of his brownest paw and sat in awe.

Kipper was speechless with enchantment. It was so beautiful, so dainty, so trusting, so lovable. He must give it a name worthy of such a delectable pet. He thought hard, then the perfect name came to mind. He would call her Ruby.

This time he was making no mistakes. Ruby must never get swept up, soaked by the rain, run over by a bicycle. He had to find Ruby a safe home. He knew where there were some empty jam jars but the logistics of keeping her in a glass cylinder were beyond him. He had acquired an empty matchbox, but if he put Ruby in it then he wouldn't be able to see her, and what was the point of having a pet you couldn't see?

Suddenly he had a brilliant idea.

"You must come and see this," said Jo from an upstairs window. "Kipper's doing a weird walk."

"It's a John Cleese impersonation," said her other half.

"He's going into the greenhouse. How odd."

"As long as he doesn't sit on my seedlings."

Kipper was indeed doing a weird walk. It required the utmost concentration to keep Ruby balanced on his brownest paw and at the same time propel them both towards the greenhouse. Finally he made it, limbs aching, tail tired out with maintaining a fine balance. He deposited his precious burden on to a seed tray of lobelia. Ruby looked around with interest, impressed by her new blue and fragrant quarters, whirled her gauzy fans and settled down to find supper. She was not called the farmer's friend for nothing.

Kipper gazed at her in rapt adoration. He wondered if she could play and, joy of joys, she took off for a genteel skimming and whizzing around inside the greenhouse. Kipper pranced and leaped, patting the air. He could hardly give her a great whack as he had the fast-food bag. In payment for his carefulness, she was so loving, returning time and time again to tread the jungle of his fur with tiny, tickly feet.

I must seem like a giant to her, he thought, dazed and bemused.

He brought her things to eat ... a cold sausage, a mole, one of Jo's bras. Ruby looked at them politely and stuck to her diet of greenfly and scale-insects. She wasn't even interested in a live frog, carried with infinite care in Kipper's jaws.

"What has got into Kipper now?" said Joe. "He's sitting in the greenhouse wearing a look of smug contentment with a ladybird perched on his head."

"Ecology," said her other half. "He's joined the green movement."

Kipper was filled with satisfaction. His plan of keeping Ruby in the greenhouse was saving her from the miniature battlefield he knew

existed out there in the meadow. It was a hor-
rendous minefield of predators lying in wait for
other insects, and Ruby had very little in the
way of defense. Her natural camouflage was her
main asset. The bright colors could startle a
predator and give her time to get away. She
could also exude a caustic fluid if that failed.

She was also saved from fighting off her old
enemy, the ant. Ants liked to milk a sweet
honey-dew liquid from aphides and they would
stand guard over a branch of greenfly, repelling all invaders. In the greenhouse, Ruby had
the greenfly to herself. Even Jo noticed the
difference.

"The tomato crop is going to be splendid this
year," she said.

Kipper liked to believe that he and Ruby
could communicate by means of her wings beat-
ing at a specific rate. He tried to imitate the
sound with a thin, vibrant growling. It was no
sillier than Jo saying "Miaow, miaow" to him
as she often did.

After breakfast one morning, Kipper hurried
out to play with his pet, but something alerted
his sensitive antennae. He was soon picking up
distress signals. He raced to the greenhouse.
Ruby was lying on her back, six tiny legs
thrashing the air. Kipper looked at her,
appalled. What on earth was the matter? Was
she having a fit?

Kipper padded around helplessly, sniffing at
his distraught pet. He tapped her shell tentatively but Ruby recoiled as if in agony.

There was no doubt Ruby needed help and

urgently. Jo would know what to do. They were always giving each other pills up at the house if they had a headache or a tummy upset. Perhaps Ruby had a tummy upset. He could see her tummy and she was certainly upset. Sometimes they tried to give him a pill but he was a dab paw at finding them in his food or spitting them out later. He usually hid them behind the boiler or under the refrigerator.

Perhaps they would take Ruby to the vet's. Kipper's heart fell. He could not bear the thought of his darling in that chilly white place with its antiseptic smell and clinical atmosphere. How was he to get Ruby to the house? There was no way he was going to be able to hop across the garden with Ruby on the point of expiring. He needed some kind of stretcher. Ruby solved the problem herself with a convulsion that shot her on to a fallen leaf, still on her back, legs whizzing like electric fans.

Kipper dragged the leaf slowly up to the house. It seemed to take hours of skillful maneuvering, over the lawn, along the path, up the steps and into the house. He stopped in the cool darkness of the hall, panting with nervous tension, and miaowed plaintively for Jo to come and help.

"Good heavens, what have you brought in?" said Jo. "I hope it's not a dead mouse." Then she laughed. "Look, Kipper has brought in a ladybird. How sweet."

She tipped the leaf over into the palm of her hand and the ladybird landed upright. She shook out her wings and slowly investigated the new sensation of clean, smooth-textured skin.

Jo went to the doorway. "Ladybird, ladybird, fly away home," she chanted. "Your house is on fire and your children alone."

She shook her hand into the air and the ladybird took off. For a moment she was a tiny red dot flying, then she was away over the hedge and gone.

Kipper sat on the floor in shock. It was all over. He couldn't believe it. His Ruby had gone. Their idyll was shattered. He sat completely still, the cold world of loneliness washing over him, not knowing what to do.

"Would you like some milk, Kipper?" Jo asked. There was no response. "Please yourself then."

Some time later he forced himself to stir. He wandered round the garden, dazed, looking nostalgically at the spot where they had first met. He couldn't go into the greenhouse, the memories were too painful.

Of course, if Ruby's house was on fire and her children alone, then she had to go home, he told himself. He did not question how Jo knew. He just hoped Ruby was in time and not reduced to a cinder.

He went off his food, wandering around, not taking an interest in life at all. He knew he ought to get another pet. But he didn't want anything else; he only wanted Ruby.

It was a hot, damp morning when she suddenly reappeared on the branch of a rose bush. He leaped up to greet her but she flew off, alarmed. Then he spotted her again—and again, here, then there. She was flitting about everywhere. He chased after her, his long brown speckled fur streaming in the warm breeze.

Startled, it dawned on Kipper that there were two ladybirds in the garden, no . . . there were three, four. Which was Ruby? Had she brought her children with her? Were they all homeless? Well, there was plenty of room in the greenhouse.

He bounced joyfully over the lawn, herding them together. Four pets! It was just a question of getting them used to the idea. He was confident of being successful . . . eventually.

Jo's other half watched Kipper's antics from a window. "That cat's gone crazy," he said morosely. "I blame his name. This wouldn't be happening if you'd called him something sensible like Fluffy."

SOCKAHOLIC

When Polly came out of hospital she was somewhat alarmed to be given a get-well present of a man's navy blue sock from her little cat, Dover. She wondered if he had become unbalanced by her sudden disappearance to Bellamy Ward and being abandoned to the inexperienced care of her neighbors.

"How very sweet," she said, giving him a hug and a kiss. "I suppose you do know that this isn't a mouse? Never mind, it's the thought that counts. Are you pleased to have me home? I didn't mean to go away, Dover. It was the ice."

Dover's deep purr and ecstatic twistings round her good ankle told her that he had already forgotten any unhappiness and was delighted to have her home. He watched her as she limped into the kitchen, holding on to the wall with one hand and using a stick with the other. She looked pale and frail, dark hair tied back in a ponytail, one foot encased in a lump of white rock.

"It was no fun, I can assure you, Dover, but I couldn't help it. I slipped on a pavement and broke my ankle. Look at this horrid plaster. It's really going to cramp my style."

Polly made a cup of tea and poured a saucer of milk for Dover. She sat down thankfully. She had assured the doctor that she would be all right on her own, but even getting into the house from the taxi had been an effort.

Dover brought her the sock again and laid it reverently at her foot. The sock was quite clean even if slightly damp.

"Now where did you get this from?" Polly tried not to scold her pet when he was obviously trying to please her. "You ought to take it back. There's some poor man with only one sock."

Dover wore his blankest expression. He had quite a repertoire of expressions, all put to good use on different occasions.

The next morning he appeared with an identical sock as Polly negotiated bumping downstairs on her bottom, the plaster foot sticking out in front of her.

"Going up was even funnier," she assured the cat. Then she saw the sock dangling from his jaws. "Now that's naughty, Dover. Have you turned into a delinquent while I've been away?"

Dover practiced a menacing growl, dropped the sock at her feet then sat on the floor to clean his whiskers before breakfast. The elderly couple next door had been kind to him but they did not understand punctuality.

Polly put the two socks together. They were identical in color and size. She folded them neatly, tucking one ribbed top over the other.

"How about returning these?" she suggested hopefully.

Dover launched himself into the demolition of his food, pretending not to understand. Polly put the socks in an empty biscuit box on a shelf and forgot all about them. She never ate biscuits anyway. Three days later, a yellow sock with a bright diamond pattern appeared.

"What dreadful taste," she said, consigning the sock to the box. "He deserved to lose that one."

Its equally startling mate arrived on the mat the following morning. Dover looked smug. He obviously regarded these as prize specimens. Polly put it in the box without saying a word. Perhaps she was only encouraging him in this ridiculous new pastime with her speculative remarks.

She had had Dover for three years and he had never shown signs of eccentricity before. It must have something to do with her sudden hospital stay. Dover was a small, handsome cat, cobby in stature, with short white fur as thick as a carpet and amazingly big eyes which could outstare anyone. This was often disconcerting as one eye was a liquid amber color and the other the palest blue.

By the time there were five pairs of socks in her biscuit box plus two odd ones, Polly was beginning to get worried. There was a man somewhere in the area with cold feet or an astronomical sock bill. It was an estate of small Victorian terraced houses built when the railways first threw out their iron tentacles. Most of the householders were young working couples who tumble-dried and did not hang out so much as a handkerchief. There were a few elderly folk who had lived in their narrow, ornate houses all their lives and did not want to move now. They still hung out the washing but were constantly pottering about their gardens, keeping an eye open for marauding cats and encroaching flocks of magpies.

Polly was an in-between. She had bought her little house before prices soared, and was very happy there. She lived alone with her cat, quite contentedly, making a reasonable living illustrating children's books and magazine stories. The bigger of the two bedrooms had been turned into a studio so that Polly could work at home, making regular sorties to the city to see art editors and publishers.

She was decidedly worried when she had to find a second box for Dover's sock collection. The total now was nine matching pairs and four odd ones. She felt sure they belonged to the same man as they were all the same size. She began to imagine what he might be like. Blue was obviously his favorite color, with gray a close second. He was neat and methodical in his ways (apart from being careless with socks) and conservative in his choice of clothes (apart from the hideous yellow pair). He had slim feet of average size, so he was not a burly six-footer with muscles like a gorilla. It seemed he never wore brown or black, so perhaps he was fair with blue eyes. He was undoubtedly very clean.

"This is ridiculous," said Polly as Dover trotted upstairs to her studio with a pale gray silk sock. Then she stopped. "Silk . . . now he'll be really mad. These are expensive socks. Not your everyday three-packers from a chain store."

Her heart skipped a beat fractionally. Gray silk were wedding socks. So he had just got married. Next, a tumble dryer would be delivered to the house, and that would put a stop to Dover's antics. Polly sighed, half regretfully. It had been amusing to think about the owner of the socks but also embarrassing. She had even found herself glancing at men's feet in case she caught sight of someone wearing only one sock.

Her own feet were back to normal now, the plaster cast consigned to the dustbin.

For two weeks there were no more socks. He was either away on his honeymoon or the tumble dryer had arrived. Dover looked quite forlorn. He had enjoyed his life of crime. Mice and spiders were tame by comparison.

One morning Polly heard an odd muffled noise and ran downstairs. Dover could barely drag his latest captive through the cat flap. He was purring loudly with pride at his achievement. It was a soaking wet gray wool doubleribbed knee-length thermal sock.

"Mountaineering or outward bound," said Polly with interest. Perhaps she had been wrong about the wedding. No one in their senses would take a bride mountaineering.

Polly wondered if she ought to go to the police and confess. Surely by now the man had reported a sock thief. But the more she thought about it, the more unlikely it seemed. The police would probably laugh and label her a dotty artist. Perhaps it would be better if she did her own detective work.

That night Polly pretended to go to bed. Then she dressed in a warm track suit, anorak and sneakers. Armed with a torch, she followed Dover, not through the cat flap, but opening the door carefully a few moments later.

Dover was the perfect cat to follow. His distinctive white shape showed up in the dark. For a long time he seemed content to do absolutely nothing, staring up at the frosty moon while Polly froze against a wall. Then he went into a neighbor's garden and did some moongazing. It all took hours and Polly was like an icicle by the time she gave up and thawed out in a hot bath.

The next morning Dover dragged in a second mountaineering sock and laid it at her feet with a superior, knowing look.

"This has got to stop," she said firmly.

Polly decided to advertise in the local paper. There was a limit to how many socks a man could buy in a year. Besides, she was running out of boxes.

Newly married sockless mountaineer will hear something to his advantage if he contacts Box No . . .

There were a few jokey replies but no one sounded desperate for socks. He was obviously a man who did not read the small ads, but Polly did not feel that the return of twelve pairs of second-hand socks and eight odd ones merited paying for a full-page advertisement.

She toured the local sock shops. "I know this sounds odd, but do you know of a man who buys an awful lot of socks?" she asked.

The assistant's blank look out-blanked even Dover's most inane expression. Polly gave up this line of enquiry.

It was while she was illustrating a book of fairy tales that she thought of Cinderella. Though Polly flatly refused to go round knocking on doors to try socks on men's feet, she could take a leaf out of Prince Charming's book.

In her biggest scrolling script she wrote, "DOES THIS SOCK FIT?" on the back of a misty illustration of Venice. No one wrote romances set in Venice any more so she had not sold the picture.

She hung the sign in her ornate Victorian porch and stapled the mountaineering sock to a corner. Later that day she caught Dover eyeing the sock and calculating the jump factor.

"No," she warned. "You leave it alone. That sock's mine."

Someone coughed. "No, actually that sock's mine. I've brought along the feet to prove it. And the boots."

A tall, fair-haired young man with glasses was holding a pair of muddy mountaineering boots. "I haven't had time to clean them," he apologized.

"Too busy buying socks?" Polly said.

He looked bemused. "I've only just got back. The Western Highlands of Scotland. Such rugged mountains."

"Did you take your bride?"

A wary look came into his blue eyes. "I beg your pardon?"

"The wedding? You've been to a wedding recently?"

"My sister's." His eyes darkened with interest. "Are you clairvoyant?"

"If you'd like to come in for a moment, I'll explain," said Polly. "Actually, Dover should explain, but from the stubborn look on his face, he's not talking to anybody this evening."

The young man followed her into the kitchen. Dover stared at him unblinkingly from the windowsill. Polly took down the boxes and tipped the socks on to the kitchen table. The pairs were all neatly rolled up.

"Am I to believe that you have been . . . collecting my socks?"

"No, Dover has. He's become a sockaholic. I don't know if there is a cure. One had a hole in it," Polly added. "I mended it for you."

"Thank you," said the young man humbly.

"It was the least I could do."

"I suppose in a way it's my own fault. My name's Ian Cameron and I've recently moved into the corner house. I come home very late from college and do my washing in the evening. Then I rush off to work in the morning, forgetting to bring it in. Sometimes my washing is out for days, alternately wet and dry, according to the weather."

"Dover obviously thought he was operating a rescue service for abandoned socks," said Polly, wishing she had some biscuits. Ian Cameron was as slim as a reed; in too much of a rush to eat, either, it seemed. "I'm at home all day. I could bring your washing in for you."

"Would you really?" The young man had a long, slow smile that made Polly's heart turn over. She was suddenly quite moved by his gratitude. "That would be such a help."

Ian picked up the yellow pair. "Your cat can keep these. I won them in a raffle."

Polly stood on tiptoe in the porch to unstaple the mountaineering sock. He reached behind her and lifted down the sign.

"Venice," he said, with an admiring look at both painting and painter. "That's a lovely picture."

"I can't sell it," she said. "No one writes stories about Venice these days. Too much pollution and flooding."

"Could I buy it? I haven't much furniture yet. A picture would be a great improvement."

"Dover would like you to have it as a peace offering for having to buy all those new pairs of socks," said Polly.

Dover looked indignantly over his shoulder. He wanted nothing of the sort. He was not apologizing for anything. His amber eye managed to look fierce while his blue eye was icy cold.

"Dover is an unusual name for a cat," said

Ian Cameron, going over to the windowsill to stroke the enigmatic white head. Dover stared blankly. He knew they were talking about him.

"White cliffs," said Polly, happy that she had met an intellectual who would understand immediately.

"Suitably majestic," he said, not minding the white hairs brushing on to his suit sleeve as Dover began to thaw.

She'd be a fool to let such a pleasant man drift out of her life, Polly thought as she made coffee. Cinderella always had a few cards up her sleeve. Perhaps she could leave the odd sock hanging on the line for Dover. It seemed a pity to spoil all his fun.

AUNT SARAH

Aunt Sarah stood braced against the wind on the roof of the skyscraper office block and wondered how she had got there. She had been in the building several times before, but never this high.

The sudden nearness of London's rooftops and sky life was unnerving. They certainly put up some strange-looking buildings these days. A helicopter swung across at eye-level, the rays of the setting sun glinting on its beetle-black body, the rotor blades as noisy as an outraged wasp.

A fire escape door slammed shut behind Aunt Sarah. She was not too alarmed by this. Doors were always slamming on her. It was not at all unusual.

She walked tentatively to the edge of the roof

and peered over. She had only come into the office block to find her friend, each floor taking her further and further into strange territory. Perhaps her friend was not in today.

She peered over the edge again. The cars below looked just like insects. People were indistinguishable. No one knew where she was; nor was anyone likely to be looking for her. Tomorrow, about breakfast time, someone might notice her non-appearance.

"Has anyone seen Aunt Sarah?" they would ask.

She had lived at the home for nearly six years. They did not really know her, and they would not know where to begin to look for her. Her description would fit a hundred Aunt Sarahs.

She was surprised by the debris on the windy rooftop; leaves and paper wrappers scattering about; seedpods, feathers, droppings. The roof had a life of its own, but there was nothing of much interest to Aunt Sarah.

She took time arranging her coat and sat down on a low wall to think. The thoughts that filtered through her mind were comforting; she remembered the long sweet grass of her youth, a baby that suckled close to her warm body, crackling winter fires, cool summer nights when she had shared her endless dreams with the moon. Where had her youth gone? Nothing happened to her now, except being stuck on a rooftop.

The first chill of evening touched her face and she shivered. She could not stay there much longer. It was foolish. The offices in the block were beginning to close, but she could not reach any window to attract attention. She tried calling but she was well out of earshot of anyone, and her voice sounded small and distant. They probably had this double glazing anyway.

She called again, but the sound was carried away on the wind. It was obvious that no one was coming to find her.

Aunt Sarah began to panic. She had to get off the roof. The fire escape door was quite fast. She could not find another. There were few options open to her. She could not endure that high, inhospitable place a moment longer. The wind had become biting, stinging. She would have to gather her courage, take the plunge and put her trust in some kind of survival. She closed her eyes tight, took a deep breath, and then stepped off the roof.

The descent was frighteningly slow, rather like being suspended, like a high-altitude, low-opening free fall might be. The wind buffeted her face, filling her ears with uncanny sounds; windows flashed against her eyelids, though she did not see the startled faces looking up from their desks. It was far better not to look. She had disappeared before their expressions changed.

The ground was coming up to meet her now. Red blobs became buses, jagged green shapes became trees, the cityscape sharpened into familiar objects.

She came to a stop with a jolt and opened her eyes. The pavement was only an amazing few feet below. She stepped hesitatingly on to the rough tarmac roof of the single-story shopping center with shaking legs. She could not believe her luck. She was all in one piece and everything seemed to work. It was a miracle.

"Cor, did you see that?" said Joe, the younger of the window cleaners, scratching his head. "Bless me, what a joker. Well, I never. Who'd have believed it?"

"What did you say, Joe?" Arthur's mind was on fish and chips for supper, the latest episode of *Dynasty*, the darts match at the pub that evening. Joe was a conveyor-belt talker and sometimes Arthur did not bother to listen properly.

They began dismantling the cradle for the night, stacking the cleaning materials and making the slack fast. It was a good job, cleaning high-rise windows, thought Arthur, still only half listening to Joe. It was almost like traveling. He saw the world from up there.

"Didn't you see it?" Joe repeated, grinning. "Stone me if I'm not as sober as a judge. Large as life. And what a nerve! Didn't you notice we've had a passenger on the way down? Cripes, a cat, a damned great black cat."

Aunt Sarah lifted her dark face to another day with silent thanks and leaped down on to the pavement with one agile bound. Without a backward glance, she vanished into the evening rush hour crowds.

If she hurried, she might get to the home in time for supper. It was tuna tonight. Then she would watch the box with the other old ladies. Nothing ever happened any more.

MAN PHOBIA

Lucy had been treading broken glass for weeks in case she woke up and found that Mark Telford was only a beautiful dream. After years of going out with SLOBS (Sadly Lacking in anything Outstanding Blokes), Mark had walked into her life and a dismal wintery day suddenly broke into sparkling sunshine.

He was everything a girl could want. Tall, good-looking, strong and gentle, intelligent, thoughtful ... Lucy imagined that such men only existed in books. But here he was, breathing and talking to her as if she mattered. He had arrived at her office with a warm but hesitant smile that could have shattered a meter maid at ten paces.

"Miss Lucy Wilson? Really? You're much

too pretty to be editing a stuffy volume on electronics."

"There's more to editing than just reading a book," said Lucy, struggling to keep her mind on her work. "Please come in, Mr. . . . Mr. . . . ?"

"Mark Telford. *The History of the Facsimile Industry: A Hundred and Forty Years of Electronic Evolution.*"

"We ought to find a better title," said Lucy, recovering her composure and mentally tidying her emotions. "I have your manuscript here and we are all very enthusiastic about it. It does need a little lightening in places . . ."

"You mean it's boring?"

"No, not in the least. I've read it, truly. And even as a layman . . . layperson," she corrected quickly, "it was perfectly understandable. We feel . . . I feel that it needs a few photographs, line drawings, diagrams to break up the solid pages of text."

Mark Telford breathed a big sigh of relief and settled his rangy frame more comfortably in the visitor's chair. "And I thought you were going to throw two years' work back at me with a polite thank-you-very-much."

By then, Lucy already knew that she would be incapable of throwing anything back at him, except perhaps her phone number and the key to her flat. She tried to concentrate but the typing danced on the pages and all she could see was his square jaw, the crinkly laughter lines round his gray eyes, the way his hair fell forward, the warm and generous curve to his mouth.

The editorial meeting stretched into lunch, then reluctantly they had to part, but not before Mark had that phone number and they arranged to meet. Their romance blossomed with all the hallmarks of a happy ending. They enjoyed the same food, music, books, films; they laughed a lot. He never put a foot wrong. He did not fondle or grope or take it for granted that a meal ticket entitled him to a kiss. It was all so refreshingly different from SLOBS that Lucy half expected Mark to disappear one day in a puff of extra-terrestrial smoke. Someone so perfect must come from another planet.

It went without saying that one day they would live together. They both knew it. Words were not necessary. It was just inevitable. The first evening that Lucy took Mark home to her London flat, they climbed the stairs hand in hand, not knowing that the idyll was about to burst.

"I hope you're not allergic to cats," said Lucy. "I have a beautiful Abyssinian called Lagash. Not just a pet, you understand, but my dearest friend and companion for years."

"Lagash?"

"It's one of the twelve great Sumerian cities built between 3600 and 3400 B.C. I thought an elegant Abyssinian deserved an historically fitting name, something from one of the first civilizations."

"Don't worry, I like cats, especially ancient breeds. We've always had animals at home."

Lucy unlocked the door to her top-floor two-roomed flat. "That's all right then. Lagash is very special to me. Come in. It's rather small but it's home."

It was small. It was all Lucy could afford in an accessible part of London. The front door opened straight into the sitting room, which had just enough space for a two-seater settee, television, coffee table, desk and bookcase. She bustled into a matchbox-size kitchen, where everything could be reached at an arm's length. Mark glimpsed an equally minuscule bathroom.

"Small is the operative word," he said, trying to fit his long legs under the coffee table. "I may have to open a window so I can take off my jacket."

Lucy laughed. "Make friends with Lagash while I put the percolator on."

She heard him making tentative advances. "Hello, Lagash ... Come and say hello." She smiled to herself. Tall and big as he was, Mark looked so right in her flat and he was obviously making himself at home.

He ambled into the kitchen and rested an elbow on the top of the microwave. "Is there something wrong with your cat?" he asked. "Is he paralyzed or something?"

Lucy looked puzzled and brushed past him into the sitting room. "Lagash? Of course not. What's the matter?"

Lagash was crouched in a corner of the room, every limb as stiff as a poker, large amber eyes staring at Mark. Lagash was a handsome ruddy-brown Abyssinian, his ticked fur with the distinctive short dark bands along each hair. He was sleekly neat, his large pointed ears not perked at that moment with intelligence or curiosity, but laid back in sheer fright.

"Good heavens, how extraordinary," said Lucy, going down on her knees to her cat. "I've never seen him like this before. Don't be silly, Lagash. Mark won't hurt you."

Lagash did not relax even a centimeter at the sound of Lucy's coaxing voice. He was totally rigid.

"Would you mind going into the bedroom for a moment?" Lucy asked, indicating the fourth door. Mark stifled a sigh; it was not quite the invitation he had hoped for. Lucy's bedroom was neat and tidy, flower-sprigged and with hardly room to swing a . . . Sunday supplement.

"Anything to oblige an Abyssinian," he murmured.

As soon as the bedroom door shut, Lagash leaped into Lucy's arms and tried to burrow under her jersey. She could feel his little heart pounding with fear. He had been genuinely scared of Mark, but she could not think why. He had never reacted to any of her other friends. She stroked his soft russet fur, under his chin and behind his ears, all his favorite places. "There, there, you are a daft thing. You can come out, Mark. Lagash is all right now."

But Lagash wasn't. As Mark walked into the sitting room, Lagash let out a fierce yelp and froze on Lucy's lap as if Mark was a ferocious monster.

"I'm terribly sorry," said Lucy, embarrassed and upset, seeing their evening going down the drain, if not their entire future together. "He's never behaved this way before. I can't understand it. Lagash has quite a bossy nature usually."

"Something about me that he doesn't like," said Mark.

"Would you mind going into the bathroom for a few minutes?"

"With pleasure. I have exhausted the view from the bedroom."

Lucy consoled her cat and calmed him down, but each time Mark reappeared, Lagash went into his extraordinary anti-social impersonation of a pillar of salt.

Mark downed his coffee at speed. "I think I get the message. I'd better go."

"But Mark, we were going to talk ... you know, discuss the future," said Lucy, near to tears.

"What future?" said Mark with a trace of bitterness as he disappeared down the stairs. "Lagash is on to a winning streak."

Lucy dripped tears on to Lagash's big pointed ears. He nuzzled up to her, knowing that in some way he was at fault. He had let her down but was unable to understand why. His brown paws, glowing with shades of russet, kneaded her lap, and after several tramplings he curled up and went to sleep, his pale apricot underparts heaving deeply with contentment.

"Why couldn't you have behaved like this when Mark was here?" she said sadly. "You traitor. You've nearly ruined everything. You'd better be more sociable tomorrow."

But Lagash's behavior was even more erratic.

He not only froze at the sight of Mark but emitted a panic-stricken screech that sent shivers up and down Lucy's spine. Her overwrought imagination wondered wildly if perhaps Mark was, after all, a supernatural being and her cat had recognized it. Or did he have a split personality, and Lagash saw the other, sinister side?

"Bedroom or bathroom?" Mark asked with resignation.

"Would you mind the roof for a few minutes? I didn't have time to clean up this morning."

"It *is* raining."

"I'll lend you an umbrella."

Some time later that evening, Mark took her hand gently. "This isn't going to work, Lucy," he said. "Your cat has a phobia about me and I can see that you love him dearly. I'm not the sort of person to come between a woman and her cat."

"I'll think of something," said Lucy desperately. "Just give me a chance."

"Call me," he said, going down the stairs.

During the next few frantic days, Lucy called anyone or anything that was to do with cats and explained the problem. It was a trail that was littered with advice to change her boyfriend, change her cat, shut Lagash in a different room (not stipulating for how long), get a second cat. The editing of Mark's book suffered many delays.

She was nearly at her wits' end when she was referred to a Dr. Barnabas. She dialed the long string of numerals with trembling fingers.

"Dr. Barnabas's office," said a nasal twang. "Can I help you?"

"I have a cat with a phobia," Lucy began for the hundredth time.

"You've come to the right place, lady."

It said much for Mark's affection for Lucy that he agreed to face the Abyssinian once more. He could not see a way round the problem.

"Please, I want you to do exactly what I tell you," said Lucy, as they climbed the stairs. "It's very important."

"Do you want me to stand on one leg? Make noises like a sardine? Pretend to be a dead cushion?"

"Something like that. I've managed to get some advice from a doctor trained in feline behavioral problems. We have to be patient and help Lagash get over his phobia."

"So I am a phobia."

"Like spiders, snakes and crawling things are for people." Lucy could see this was not improving matters. She had to repair the damage quickly before the expression of retreat set on his face. "Apparently, it's a combination of your size and the smallness of the flat. Please do what I tell you."

They went into her flat. One alarmed look at Mark and Lagash froze to the spot. Mark looked at Lucy in despair; it seemed their romance was going to be beaten by a neurotic cat, a funny brown creature with big ears.

"Now, don't move, not one inch," Lucy hissed with clipped authority. She went in, leaving Mark standing in the doorway, six foot of immobile manhood rooted to the spot by the terrified gaze of one small sleek Abyssinian. "Don't move a muscle."

"How long do I have to stay here like this?"

"For as long as it takes," said Lucy. "Wait until you see a degree of relaxation in Lagash's body, then you can move one step."

"One step?"

"Only one step, then you must stop again. It's a case of getting Lagash conditioned to accept you so that he does not feel threatened by your presence."

"How long is this going to take?" Mark asked with resignation. "My right foot is going to sleep."

"It can't be hurried. We must go by the book. It's worth it, isn't it? Try counting."

"Up to ten?"

"Up to a hundred and then backwards."

Minutes later . . . "Seventy-four, seventy-three, seventy-two . . ." The merest flicker went through Lagash's beautiful tail. Something had relaxed.

"Move one step to the settee and sit down," said Lucy quietly.

Mark groaned with relief, especially when Lucy sat beside him and he counted to several hundred without any trouble at all.

"The psychologist said the trauma was probably caused by you suddenly filling a very small space that normally was Lagash's domain. It was his territory and you threatened it."

"You've been to see a psychologist about your cat?" Mark said incredulously.

"Not exactly. I phoned him up. He lives in New York and he's the top cat and dog psychologist. He was sorry he couldn't make a house call."

Mark closed his arms round Lucy and smoothed back her tousled hair. Lagash leaped behind the television set and froze.

"There! You see what happens? Better keep still," Lucy whispered.

"Willingly," he said against her ear.

It took several weeks of therapy and phone calls to New York before Lagash finally became accustomed to Mark's presence and size. Each time Mark arrived at the flat, he kept completely still until Lagash had relaxed, then only moved again with slow, measured, unhurried movements. Gradually Lagash accepted that the man giant was not about to flatten him against a wall. One day Mark caught Lagash actually looking at him with a degree of intelligent interest in his unblinking amber eyes.

"Don't you think it's time to call a truce?" said Mark, going down on one knee. "I'm tired of playing statues. We've both had enough of this nonsense. Come over and meet me."

Lagash sauntered sideways as if he actually intended to go the other way. He regarded the man curiously, peering closely into his face. The eye-to-eye confrontation lasted no more than a second, then Lagash arched his back and stretched, the broken necklace of marks round his neck quivering.

"Miaow," he said bossily.

"Hello to you too, buster," said Mark.

When the envelope arrived from British Telecom, Lucy whisked it out of sight. She paid the astronomical phone bill without a qualm. It was a small price for keeping both man and cat, each infinitely precious, each necessary to her world.

"I have thought of another solution," said Mark, rigid in the doorway as usual, waiting for Lagash to relax.

"What's that?"

"We could move into a larger flat."

Lagash pricked up his ears. Moving? Even hearing the word manufactured new stress symptoms. There was definitely a phobia about moving. His psychologist would know.

THE WELL-READ DRAGON

It was an ordinary winter's day when Rufus first met the dragon. The garden had been transformed overnight and the ice-laden shrubbery and flurries of snow held a magical quality of no-man's-land. Rufus was both entranced and appalled.

The scattering of snowflakes was an enticement to leap and play; the coldness of the snow beneath the soft pads of his paws was decidedly unpleasant. He leaped into the air as the Japanese maple shed its fairy raiment then lost his direction and landed nose high in a drift.

He lashed his long tail in anger. Where had his garden gone? Everything was different. He peered hard into the dazzling whiteness. The bird-table had a huge white pie on top; the rockery was a snow-capped mountain range; the paths had completely disappeared.

He plodded on, growling, sweeping his tail from side to side, determined to find out who had taken away his garden, ready for any emergency that this new world might suddenly present.

It took him several minutes to locate his regular hole in the hedge and scramble through to the meadows and the stream that meandered, fish-less, to far distant places. There was ice on the stream, floating in jagged fragments that Rufus did not trust for one instant. He crossed on the narrow bridle bridge over the stream, a little high on the magnitude of his unexpected adventure.

He knew lots of places where he could curl up and keep warm before returning for his evening meal. But it was harder to find his secret hideaways today. They had all moved. He grew colder, stumbling over hidden roots, falling into drifts, his long coat becoming frosted and bedraggled. At this rate he would have to return and sit outside the front door in the hope it was what they called the weekend and he would be allowed in to dry off on the boiler.

His long whiskers drooped in misery. He was a solitary cat. He sat for hours on windowsills, staring into the distance. They thought such remoteness denoted strength.

"Rufus is the strong, silent type," they often said.

They did not know it stemmed from shyness, an excruciating shyness that sometimes inhibited Rufus from even investigating an ant or a spider in case he was rebuffed. It was a handicap he strove to hide from his fellow creatures.

His whiskers swept forward. There was a definite rise in temperature somewhere not too far away. He sniffed around. It was not a familiar heat smell, in fact it was like nothing he had ever encountered before. He crept along on all fours, oblivious of getting his tummy wet, intrigued by this new phenomenon. The undergrowth was thick and weighted with snow as he slid into a dense tangle of broken boughs unmoved since the October storm.

The warmth was definitely closer. Rufus wondered hopefully and illogically if someone was having a barbeque or a bonfire. He fancied a burnt pork chop or a sizzled sausage.

Suddenly a huge wave of vibrant leaping fire swept towards Rufus, singeing his whiskers and sending him tumbling down a slippery rubble-filled slope into a cave.

"Well, well, well," boomed a harsh, grating voice. "What have we got here? I do believe it's an orange mouse."

Rufus got up on to all four paws, inspected his whiskers and peered into the gloom.

"I beg your pardon," he said, gathering his dignity and forgetting to be shy. "I'm not a mouse. Don't you know a mouse from a cat?"

"They are all small furry-type things."

"I'm a ginger cat. And Persian," Rufus added with pride.

"A Persian ginger cat, eh? Prove it. Speak Persian. A few lines of those old Persian poets will do."

"I am Persian but I don't speak it," said Rufus, wishing he'd never mentioned his breed.

"Thought you couldn't. Come further forward and let me have a look at you. I've never seen a ginger cat before."

Rufus hesitated. His terrible shyness was for once overridden by curiosity and the gorgeous feeling of warmth coming from inside the cave. It must be a cave he had not discovered before.

He tiptoed forward, shaking out his long fur, the heat drying it instantly. His bones luxuriated in the waves of warmth. He had good eyesight in the dark so he was at a loss to understand why he couldn't see anything. Then he noticed an odd movement to his right, a slapping movement. It was a tail, slowly undulating but like no tail he could recognize. It was hard and ridged with horny protuberances, the end flickering with bright red tongues of flowing fire.

Rufus gulped. He had never seen such an awesome tail.

"Excuse me, but where are you?" he asked in a small voice.

"I'm up here, you fool. Look up! Above you!"

Rufus raised his head carefully. It was all darkness above, a huge darkness that blotted out any light from the fire. Gradually he made out claws either side of him, solid legs and a massive body covered in leathery scales; then a long weaving neck, ridged with horns. At the end of the weaving neck a pair of piercing green eyes blazed like beacons.

Rufus was petrified. He froze to the spot, his

heart pounding. He was standing directly beneath the creature. Any movement and he would be crushed in a fraction.

"Don't be frightened, small ginger non-Persian-speaking creature," said the voice more kindly. "It's only my appearance. After all, think how you must look to a fly, and you wouldn't hurt one, would you?"

Rufus was speechless. He would have shaken his head if he had been able to move.

"If you wouldn't mind backing off a bit, I could sit down. I'd hate to tread on you. I haven't had a visitor for three centuries and there's such a lot I want to talk about."

Rufus crawled backwards until his tail met the wall of the cave. He made himself as small as possible, flattening his fluff into the curve of the rock. The black mass above him heaved and writhed, twisting in a feline fashion till it was hunched down on all fours, its gruesome head peering closer and closer.

"My word, you are small," the monster grunted through enormous pointed fangs. "I suppose you're what's known as a toy."

"I am not a toy," Rufus hissed.

"Come now, I could bounce you around. Like a rubber ball, you'd come bouncing back to me . . ." The creature broke into ear-splitting song.

Rufus felt his hackles rise. It might be the biggest, ugliest monster he had ever seen, but he was not going to be insulted. He would sink his claws into that long nose and create quite a bit of damage, even if it was the last thing he ever did. His fur rose and a low growl came from deep in his throat as he crouched ready to spring.

"Fascinating, absolutely fascinating. You're actually contemplating an attack. Well done, midget. Come in and have a crumpet. You definitely deserve a crumpet for that."

Rufus could already smell the crumpets toasting and the butter melting in spongy holes. He loved butter desperately. He followed his nose further into the cave. The crumpets were sizzling nicely on a hot rock.

"Excuse me, sir, but would you mind telling me what you are?" Rufus asked timidly, sniffing the delicious buttery air.

"I'm a dragon! And I've been a dragon all my life. Dragon, dragon, dragon . . . say it a hundred times and it's absolutely meaningless."

The dragon stretched and roared, eyes turning from green to red, a long tongue leaping out to the crumpets. He tossed a couple down his throat with expert flips.

"Help yourself, help yourself, young fellow. Make yourself at home."

"Where do you get all these crumpets?" said Rufus, chewing a morsel, butter running down his chin.

"Some little girl in a red hood. She's always tripping about with a basket of the things, going to see her grandmother. She drops them all over the place. Terribly careless. Well, tell me what you've done today, small orange furry thing."

"Er . . ." Rufus thought hard. It had better be good. "I had a life-threatening confrontation with a marble. I won, of course, by hiding it in a wellington boot. Won't get out, you know, never."

The dragon yawned and engulfed the cave in hot air. "How fascinating. Anything else?"

"Then I attacked my people's king-sized duvet, pounding it into submission. It was exhausting," said Rufus, helping himself to more crumpet.

"And did you smite the king?" the dragon roared with a flicker of interest.

"Never saw the king," Rufus admitted. "I would have if I had seen one. What about you?" Rufus asked, detecting shaky ground and changing the subject quickly. "What have you done today?"

"Oh, I read, of course. I read all day and every day. Today I read some Tolstoy, a couple of Dickens, several Tennessee Williams plays, all of Stephen Spender's poems and a couple of Margaret Drabble novels."

"All in one day?" Rufus was impressed. He couldn't read at all, not even the labels on his cat food.

"A mere nothing. A quiet day. No damsels in distress and I haven't seen a knight for years."

Rufus did not say anything. He saw a night every day but he was not going to argue with a dragon.

"I thought I would offer myself for a part in the next *Star Wars*," the dragon went on, preening himself. But when I turned up at the audition, everyone ran away screaming. They're going to use those ridiculous mechanical tortoises on legs instead. Hardly inspired."

"How very frustrating," Rufus agreed.

"What am I doing with my life? Nothing. I'm so big and ugly. Nobody asks me out; I don't get to go to any literary lectures or writers' conferences. I suppose I could do an Open University course, but the post is so unreliable."

"I know the postman," said Rufus, on more secure ground. "I see him every morning. I could bring your post."

"A little baby thing like you? Those tutorials are pretty thick and heavy. You'd better go home now or the duvet-duo will be sending out a search party, and we don't want them to find us, do we?"

Rufus scuttled home through the snow, warm in heart and body. He had a friend, it was all that mattered. Not a particularly good-looking friend, a bit eccentric, on the large side, but a friend nevertheless. Rufus was ecstatic. He leaped over snow drifts and bounded into the garden, his tail feathering flakes like an electric fan, scattering snow through the cat flap.

She scooped him into a big towel and flattened his ears. "Who's all wet?" she whispered close to his pink nose. "Who wants his supper?"

Rufus gave a buttery hiccup. He did not have an inch of room left for supper but he would do his best. He was always a trier. The resulting indigestion nearly put him off visiting the dragon the next day, but he made his way manfully to the cave. He found the dragon wallowing in self-pity, tears pouring in fountains down his leathery cheeks.

"Look at you, orange thing," the dragon

howled. "You're so beautiful ... with the fire shining through your fur like gold dust, dear little pink nose and those long whiskers so delicate and fragile. I wish I had long whiskers to swish about ... but what about me? I'm just plain ugly."

"No, no, you do have very nice eyes ..."

"Oh, really ... do I?" the dragon smirked, flapping his lashes. "What are they like?"

Rufus tried to think of a good long word. "Eloquent."

The dragon wove his head from side to side, hissing and sighing, eyes limpid with emotion. "Eloquent ... aaah."

"My whiskers are not just for show," added Rufus, embarrassed. "They're a radar system."

"Technology! Now he blinds me with technology," the dragon wept afresh.

"It's about all I do know," said Rufus humbly.

"Good," said the dragon, mollified. "I couldn't stand a know-all for a friend. Gee, all that crying's made me hungry."

"What do you normally eat, besides crumpets?" Rufus asked nervously.

"Words, of course."

"Not cats?"

"Urgh, cats! Never touch them."

Rufus picked his way between piles of books. They were stacked in their hundreds at the back of the cave, well thumbed, well read, pages turned down, flints and dried leaves for bookmarks. "Don't you have any shelves?"

"Shelves? What are shelves? Don't all books live in piles? That's the proper way to keep books, in piles that live and grow. Them books are growing."

"Where do you get your books from? Does the mobile library come round?"

The dragon coughed up a bit of fire. "I have my sources. Sometimes authors give me original manuscripts. I've one or two nice items. I've the epic *Beowulf*, for instance, in immaculate condition. It's a bit long though, purely for reading, not eating."

The next day Rufus dragged a carrier bag full of books and magazines down to the cave. He was not going to risk any more emotional outbursts. The dragon was too big.

The dragon pounced on the Sunday supplements and flicked through to the back page. "Wonderful, I haven't read my horoscope for aeons. It says I'm going to have a good week and the Sun-Pluto angle is going to boost my psychic system! And what are all these titles? Mills & Boon? I haven't read any of these before. Any relation to Nietzsche?"

"One of my people reads them all the time. She likes them. She says they are pure escapism."

"Escapism! Bliss, exactly what I need. I've been longing to escape from this cave. You're a good friend, I really appreciate it." The dragon tossed a few down his long throat and swallowed reflectively. " 'Tall, dark and handsome, Gareth's piercing eyes lit up his craggy face with passion'—say, that describes me to a T. These are great stories, a change from Homer, Tolstoy, and Fyodor Dostoyevsky's *Crime and*

Punishment. Get me some more escaping things, orange mouse."

"Don't eat them! She has to take them back or she'll be fined. They're borrowed from the library. They're very popular."

"Sorry, just a little snack."

A strange expression came over the dragon's face, a brooding look. Rufus hoped he was not hungering for a few damsels. The dragon rocked back on his heels, a faraway look in his hooded eyes.

"Can you get me some paper?" he muttered, deep in thought. "Some plain paper?"

Rufus felt himself dismissed. A dragon, thinking, was an unknown commodity. Better lie low for a few days. He warmed his back on the dragon's brooding breath for a few seconds, then crept out of the cave. The snow had nearly gone, leaving a sullen slush that trickled endlessly down the path. He dragged his wet tail indoors, making a damp trail over the kitchen floor.

"Who's all wet?" Rufus found himself upended in a towel, his ears flattened, his tail being patted dry. "Who doesn't like the snow?"

Later, he hunted around the house for paper. He found a pack of Christmas cards, a roll of wrapping paper, a bag of toilet rolls, some half-used exercise books, a shopping pad and a packet of brown envelopes. He dragged them down the garden in another carrier bag.

As he neared the cave, Rufus became aware of a distinct change in atmosphere. It was frenetic. The dragon was not his usual calm, placid self, toasting crumpets and reading books.

Instead he was pacing the cave, a frown of concentration on his face, the floor littered with piles of crumpled paper.

"Good, good, more paper. I've used up this lot. It's not easy, this writing business ... but I've written several popular novels this morning. Would you get them off to the publishers Bills & Moon right away? I've done a lot of market research. I know exactly what they want. They want tall, dark heroes. Read this one, the hero's twenty-four feet tall."

"I don't think they mean that tall," said Rufus.

"And he's a high achiever. He's just blown up an erupting volcano, shot down the rapids, doubled his fortune in the wheat plains of Central America and put down an entire Mexican uprising single-handed."

"All in one day?" asked Rufus faintly.

"Just the morning. He would have done more if it weren't for this appalling racket going on outside. I can't concentrate for the noise. What is it, for heaven's sake?"

"It's a protest, a demonstration," said Rufus, who had heard his people talking about it. "About the new rail link to the Channel Tunnel."

"Rail link? Rail link? You mean we're going to have one of those monstrous artificial dragons on wheels, roaring and spitting fire, rumbling all over the countryside, spoiling the environment? I don't believe it. Protest ... by golly, I'll show them a real protest."

The dragon curled himself into a seething coil, sucking in the heat of the fire. The walls of the cave shuddered as he drew flames from the bowels of the earth. Rufus flattened himself behind a rock and tucked his nose under his tail. He didn't want to see this.

Suddenly the dragon let out a tremendous roar and a wave of billowing fire burst from his gaping red mouth. It soared from the cave, scorching everything in its path. Grass shriveled; trees groaned; the stream shrank into a cloud of steam, leaving the merest trickle.

Rufus shot out of the cave, bouncing across the hot earth, up the length of his garden and through the cat flap. He bounded on to the nearest lap and fluffed out his fur to cool off.

"Whatever's that awful noise?" she said curiously. "It sounds like an earthquake, but this isn't earthquake country."

The next day, Rufus dragged the morning newspaper down to the cave, drooling with excitement. The dragon had quietened down quite a bit; he was holding an icepack to his head.

"Sssh," he wailed. "I've got a terrible headache."

"You're famous, famous," said Rufus, slapping the newspaper down on the floor in front of the dragon. "Headlines in all the morning newspapers. 'Massive earth disturbance on Kent-Surrey border,' " he read. " 'Channel Rail Route now in question.' "

The dragon's piercing eyes lit up his craggy face, headache forgotten. "Massive Earth Disturbance? That's me, all right. MASSIVE EARTH DISTURBANCE," he roared. "I'm a MASSIVE EARTH DISTURBANCE!" he roared again.

Rufus flung himself against the cave wall. This was one crazy dragon.

"In all the morning newspapers, eh? Do they want to interview me?"

Rufus had learned a lot in the last few days. He knew how to handle a dragon now. "I told them you were too busy writing your memoirs. I told them to call back in another century."

"You're a splendid fellow," bellowed the dragon. "I've just had a great idea for a Twills & Coon. It's about an extremely tall business tycoon who buys up the entire earth to excavate a Round the World Tunnel. Then there's this beautiful, eloquent-eyed damsel who fights him fang and nail because she wants to save the environment for small furry orange things. What a story! Bring me some more paper, old chap."

Rufus spent the rest of the day culling paper from the household. He hid his haul under a hedge.

"Poor Rufus," said his person that evening, stroking him. "What a pity Rufus hasn't any friends. He's spent most of the day dragging bags round the garden."

Rufus miaowed in a pathetic, friendless way and she gave him the top of the milk. How could they possibly know? He had hundreds of friends now, Dickens, Tolstoy, the Brontës, Hemingway, Kipling, Maeterlinck, Twain . . . the list was endless.

And how many cats could boast of a dragon for a friend? A well-read dragon at that . . .

FORGET-ME-NOT

My initial reaction was cold fear. Don't panic, I said to myself. Breathe slowly ... two, three, four. Think calmly and make a few discreet enquiries.

I went up to the man walking in front of me.

"Excuse me, sir," I began hesitantly. "I believe you were on the same bus as me. I couldn't help noticing you because of your ... your ... h-height."

He tipped back the wide brim, revealing a pleasant but touchingly embarrassed face. "You couldn't help noticing me because of my hat," he said helpfully.

"Well, I didn't like to—"

"You may."

"What?"

"You may mention it."

I took another deep, controlling breath. I was not breaking all my personal rules about talking to strangers just to discuss his ridiculous headgear.

"I wonder if you happened to notice if I was carrying a box on the bus? It's very important. A cardboard box, tied up with string, with holes in it."

"Holes?"

"Small, medium and large."

"Valuable?"

"Priceless."

"I remember passing you on my way out but you didn't have a cardboard box with priceless holes. I did notice you but you were carrying a supermarket bag from Gateway's."

I gasped and swung round against the flow of pedestrians, apologizing for my clumsiness, whether perpetrated or not. I always find it easier to apologize in advance. The man followed me, ducking his head to accommodate his height under overhanging branches.

"I must have left the box at the supermarket," I gabbled on, feeling I owed him an explanation. "I'll have to go back before someone chucks it out with the rubbish."

"I'll come with you," the young man offered.

"No need," I said briskly. "I can find the supermarket on my own."

"Maybe, but two pairs of eyes would find your cardboard box faster. Supermarkets are piled high with such boxes, all looking alike and very confusing. Is it the store on the corner? Then I know a short cut."

He was right. Two pairs of eyes would be more efficient and I supposed I needn't look at the hat. I could keep my eyes averted. "Haven't you got anything else to do?"

"No, and I'm tired of riding on buses. It's so boring. The inactivity is slowly sapping all my creative thought."

This conversation was getting too complicated for me so I quickened my steps. The shop would be closing soon and I had to find that box. All the possible repercussions rushed in on me, adding to my distress. It was going to be bad enough when I got home.

Mrs. Mower had been reluctant from the start. My youth and inexperience were banked against me from the moment she opened her front door.

"Oh, so you're Laura Jeffries, are you?" she said. "I expected someone older. You sounded older on the phone."

"I've got a cold," I apologized.

"You'd better come in," she said. "I'm not saying yes, mind. We'll have a little talk first. I'm very particular and there's only one left."

It had taken all my powers of persuasion to convince Mrs. Mower that youth could mean enthusiasm and inexperience a willingness to learn, unshackled by bad habits. There was nothing about my appearance that spelled out seasoned daydreamer with an incorrigible tendency to walk six inches off the ground with my head in a fantasy world. I didn't tell her that I had left more umbrellas on tube trains, books on buses, purchases on counters, than any other twenty-year-old in existence.

"Late-night shopping," said the young man. "You're born lucky or they would have been closed, shop shut, rubbish dumped. Now describe this box to me in detail. Any distinguishing marks?"

I thought hard about distinguishing marks but none materialized. "Brown cardboard," I said, pausing. "White string. Holes."

"In three sizes?"

"Yes. And it might be moving."

The vague look fell from his steely gray eyes like magic. They positively glinted with interest. "A moving cardboard box? Now that really boosts the recoverability."

"I'm very glad."

He pushed me through the swing doors into the crowded supermarket. The aisles were thronged with late-night shoppers stocking up for a siege.

"Let's split," he suggested, hat bobbing. "I'll start right over at the far end; you start here. We'll sweep the aisles systematically. That way we'll cover the same area twice. Whoever finds the box stands still. The first rule on becoming lost now also applies to becoming found."

I was relieved to have this intellectual assistance despite the parade-ground style, and especially now that he and his hat were distanced to the other side of the shop. People were staring at him, amused and puzzled. I, too, began to wonder why he was wearing it. He had such

nice eyes, very Robert Redford. He probably
had matching hair . . .

I pulled myself back from the start of the day-
dream. It was daydreaming that had got me
into all this trouble. I tramped along the
stacked aisles of baked beans and spaghetti,
Diet Pepsis and mineral water, Euro Superwash
and disinfectant, trying to think where else I
had been after my visit to Mrs. Mower's house.
I simply couldn't remember. Had I posted letters, or had that been yesterday? I bought a
magazine at the newsagent's, a prescription and
sweeteners at the chemist . . . did I pop into the
library or not? My memory was in auto-spin . . .
was I ever going to be a normal person?

The hat was not moving. It was stationary,
head and shoulders above the throng, over by
pet foods. For a moment, nothing registered and
then I broke into a run, scattering shoppers and
trolleys. A wire basket was parked on the floor
beside piles of super-sized bags of litter. In it
was my cardboard box, holes and string and all.

"You didn't tell me it also makes a noise," he
said, raising his dark eyebrows.

I went down on my knees, shaking, struggling
with the string. He came to my rescue again,
tut-tutting over the granny knots. I opened the
lid and took out the soft bundle of fur, cradling
it under my chin.

"Baby, baby, baby," I crooned, near to tears.

"A Blue Burmese," he said.

I nodded proudly, stroking the bluish-gray
glossy coat with my forefinger. The kitten mewed
piteously, opening its tiny pink cavern of a

mouth. "My first kitten. Isn't she beautiful? Look at her almond-shaped oriental eyes, and she's already getting that silver sheen on her coat."

The young man got up off his knees. "It's hungry, it's frightened and it could have been thrown out," he said. "I don't wish to pass judgment but have you seriously thought whether you are fit to have a kitten? People ought to be issued with licenses with a cat-ability rating first."

"I know, I know," I said, shocked by his words, rocking back on my heels. "But I put it in the wire basket because I couldn't manage everything with two hands. I only put the box down for a second while I filled the other basket. It was so exciting buying cat food and litter and a little brush and comb. I was thinking about names for the kitten and where it would sleep, and little toys stuffed with cat-mint that I would make ... then I hurried out to pay and got on the bus ... I was daydreaming. I've dreamed so long of having my own little cat. Don't you know what it's like to long for something for years, then suddenly it happens, so unexpectedly? The world goes all funny."

He gave me a strange look. "Well, I daresay there's no harm done," he said, examining the mewing infant. "There's a café next door. We'll get some milk for the kitten, abandoned; hot sweet tea for one owner, distraught; coffee for rescuer, intrepid."

"Do you always talk so funny?" I said a little later, when I had calmed down and the kitten, full of milk, had curled into a sleepy ball on my lap, her long tail tucked over her nose. Her whiskers were twitching. Perhaps she was a daydreamer like me and was already chasing butterflies and leaves.

"No," he said. "Sometimes I talk quite normally. It's the influence of the stovepipe hat."

"I suppose you wouldn't like to tell me why you are wearing such an outrageous hat?" I asked, curiosity brimming over, so to speak. He looked like a young Lincoln, fearless and incorruptible.

He searched his pockets and brought out a crumpled sheet of paper covered in signatures. "Sponsored Hat Week. I'm wearing a silly hat every day this week. People sponsor me by the hour or by the day. It's in aid of a children's charity. I suppose," he added humbly, searching in another pocket for a pen, "you wouldn't care to sponsor me, just for an hour?"

"It's the craziest thing I've ever heard of," I smiled. "But I'd be honored."

"And I'd be honored if you would care to come to the charity ball with me next Saturday," he said in a low voice. "I'm prepared to remind you constantly, if it's something you're likely to forget."

I looked up at him and saw bits of dark hair escaping from under that hat, and thought what courage he had, to look perfectly ridiculous for the sake of a children's charity, and I remembered the way he had held my kitten in his strong hands. Daydreaming was all right for some people but perhaps it was time I came down to earth.

"I'd like that," I said. I wondered if rescuer, intrepid, was the answer for daydreamer, incorrigible. My kitten stretched tiny pin-pricking claws into the palm of my hand as I floated down from the clouds.

XIANG,
JUNGLE CAT

The October storm took the South of England by surprise. It battered the soft-edged undulating countryside without mercy, shook the ancient earth from the roots of its medieval trees and tossed them into the air like matchsticks. Hundred-mile-an-hour gusts tore out the younger saplings, bending others till their crowns touched the ground; animals fled and cowered; electricity failed; roofs lifted off and crashed on to cars.

The animals in the zoo were terrified. The howling wind sent them shivering to the back of their cages, where they found some protection and security in the familiarity of their sleeping quarters. But there was no sleep for any animal that night. They called to each other in distress as the world they knew crashed around them.

Xiang, a big jungle cat, crouched low as the wind tore through his thick fawn and black fur and flattened his long whiskers. The air was pungent with new odors as the landscape was stirred and reshaped by a giant hand. Patterns changed as whole woods and forests toppled into walls of fallen timber.

The seven-year-old Malaysian Clouded Leopard paced nervously. He was very wild and highly strung though his ancestors had endured such a climate for generations. Malaysia was a country of tropical storms and hurricanes; heavy monsoon rains regularly drenched the thick canopy of forest.

The big cat was more afraid of the unknown. The zoo was his home and the head cat keeper his friend. He wondered where the bearded man was now and if he was safe in all this wild weather. Xiang knew his own survival depended on his keeper and the staff of the zoo.

Suddenly there was a wrenching of roots and a huge tree toppled towards Xiang, its branches blackening out the sky like the wings of a monstrous crow. It was an incredible sight which terrified Xiang and froze him to the spot.

The tree crashed down, thrashing in its death throes, branches twisted and broken, twigs flying in all directions. Xiang blinked against the cloud of dust and debris, blowing nervously through his nostrils.

As the hurricane raced across the counties, leaving a trail of unbelievable devastation,

Xiang surveyed the damage to his cage. The tree had completely flattened the wire and now the wind was finishing the demolition. He looked at it curiously, half expecting his keeper to come along and straighten it out.

He clambered over the branches and walked majestically along the horizontal trunk. It felt good to be walking with such amazing freedom; fleeting memories came into his mind of jungles with dense trees and steaming foliage, of walking along such limbs, of leaping from branch to branch, of climbing great heights to find the cooler air, his claws digging into the bark.

He shook freedom into his limbs, nervousness gone, and his toes tingled with expectation. He would at least have a look around. His world had been restricted for a long time, and he had enough normal feline curiosity to wonder what lay beyond.

He trod through a wilderness of torn trees and branches, leaped over misshapen root stumps molded in mud, chased the scurrying leaves. He felt the power going out of the storm. The wind was moving away; an element with its own volition and impetuous violence, blowing itself out over another part of the land.

The air felt different, swept yet sulphurous, and rain blew into his face as he padded along a path strewn with crackling leaves, then climbed a perimeter fence and went out on to a road. It was a strange place, all these trees everywhere, lying fallen over in untidy heaps. He saw people moving about by some crushed cars and slunk back into the undergrowth, keeping his distance. He was not ready for people, especially those who were shouting to each other. He did not trust them.

Xiang roamed the Kent woods as it grew light, astonished by the devastated countryside. He had not expected the world to look like this. He had expected something like the zoo, more orderly, not this wild and wrecked landscape. It was way past his meal time and his stomach rumbled with hunger. He wanted his keeper to appear with his usual raw meat. He growled in anticipation, wondering where his long-time friend had got to. Nothing was right somehow.

His long rosette-marked tail whipped the undergrowth and a grumbling grew low in his throat. He smelt rodents and rabbits and all his hunting instincts returned. He was the wildest of the Clouded Leopards in the zoo, unlike Babacia, a beautiful female who would talk to and rub against her keeper, sometimes jumping on to his back and stretching out languorously along his spine, with implicit trust on both sides.

A Clouded Leopard's natural diet is birds and mammals, so Xiang had little trouble in getting his own food. He was somewhat out of practice at hunting, but the basic skill soon sharpened as he crouched in the undergrowth, waiting to pounce.

Later on he found a farm, but the activity frightened him. There seemed to be swarms of humans clearing up the fallen trees and branches. Xiang was used to the people at the zoo, lots of faces staring at him when they were safely the other side of his wire, but here the people were milling about with dangerous-looking implements.

"They say there's a leopard escaped from the zoo."

"And it's a wild one."

"Better keep the kids indoors."

"Don't fancy meeting forty pounds of hungry leopard head-on, not a real live one."

Part of that day Xiang slept fitfully in a barn. The door had been blown off and he found a way in. It was warm and comfortable, but he longed for the familiarity of his cage and the friendly voice of his keeper. No one had spoken to him all day and, despite his wildness, he missed the companionship of people.

His new life followed the pattern of a nocturnal animal. He hunted at night, combing the woods and farmland of Kent for rabbits and rodents. He had an uncanny, creepy feeling that he was being hunted too. Several people spotted him in the headlights of their cars, and the air became suddenly electric with their fear.

One night, to his joy, Xiang came across familiar territory. It was the zoo. He climbed the fence and walked the perimeter track, taking in all the familiar sights and sounds. His own cage was being rebuilt. He prowled round it, sniffing and rubbing; but the wildness had got into his veins, and at the sound of someone approaching, he was off in a flash, leaping over the fence with one magnificent bound.

"That's him," said a man's voice. "That was Xiang."

"Dammit. We could have got him then."

Xiang quivered with confusion. He recognized one of the voices as that of his keeper. The familiar sound brought back all sorts of longings and he was torn by conflicting desires. That voice meant security, affection, normality ... the total opposite to the weird, alien countryside Xiang found himself living in now.

"Perhaps he'll come back," said the first man, hope overlaying his own disappointment.

Xiang did go back. Now that he knew where the zoo was, he could not keep away. He was unaware that a vast hunt was being organized for him and, despite the fact that Clouded Leopards rarely attack humans, many people in the area were afraid to leave their homes.

The sleek six-foot leopard regularly walked the perimeter track of the zoo at night. He was spotted several times, slinking through the shadows, particularly close to where his old cage used to be.

They set a trap baited with a dead chicken.

Xiang walked innocently into the trap. The chicken was polished off in no time and he curled up, strangely sleepy, then went into a deep dreamless sleep, not knowing that the keepers waited in the dark nearby.

He did not seem to be surprised when he awoke a long time later to find himself recaptured. Xiang had seen the outside world and was not impressed. He preferred the familiarity of his cage and the regular food which he did not have to catch. His streak of wildness had yearned for a dense and steaming jungle that existed thousands of miles away, not the temperate Kent countryside.

He growled at his keeper, knowing him, and there was no threat in the sound. It was the nearest the Clouded Leopard could get to a purr, a wild, untamed purr that said he was glad to be home.

He shook freedom from his long, sensuous body and settled for the life he knew.

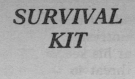

SURVIVAL KIT

Coming home to an empty house was the worst part of being alone. The rooms echoed with nothingness. The only sound was the breathing of flowers, faded, drooping, but not quite ready for the bin. Much like her, in fact.

How strange the bed looked, lop-sided. One side smooth and untouched; the other side with her floral nightie neatly folded and the pile of paperbacks with which she anaesthetized herself each night. The bathroom floor was unfamiliarly dry; no damp patches, no hair clippings, no discarded towels and pants, no rim round the bath.

No coat on the banisters, no ties on door handles, no newspapers on the floor. Everywhere was so tidy.

She stood motionless at the kitchen window, waiting for the kettle to boil, staring at a garden she hardly recognized. Snow on daffodils. It was freak weather. There had been a spell of warmth which had brought out the spring flowers, then a sudden drop in temperature with leaden gray skies and icy flakes which bit unprotected skin like small teeth. Much like him. He had been freak weather.

She still counted in days. Sixteen days now since he had left her. At first, shocked and in crippling pain, she had made a list of the things she wanted to do: go to the theater, make trips to the sea, museums and exhibitions, use her unexpected freedom. So far she had done nothing.

"I must organize myself," she said as she stirred the tea.

She found a bill addressed to both of them and crossed his name out. She wrote on it: *1) Evening Classes. 2) Eat Out. 3) New Hairstyle.* But the words bounced off the paper and she was left with the dread of being lost and never being properly alive again.

Work was as automatic as breathing. She arrived at the office on time, typed, answered the phone, made coffee, programmed herself to cope, make the right replies, compose her office face.

But at home it was different. He had left space. The television was meaningless mouthings and the radio merely background noise. She heard nothing and her sight was still unfocused. The snow swirled down on to the brown earth like icing sugar on a chocolate cake. There was a movement among the flurries, a small animal or a cluster of leaves. She did not like animals. Their scuttling alarmed her.

Her tea grew cold as she watched the snow thickening to a lacy blanket. The waste bin needed emptying. She went outside, bowing her head to the blizzard, watching the tips of her moccasin slippers pick up a crust of snow.

The animal was crouched against the dustbin like a small white hedgehog, blinking against the snow that stuck to its lashes. It was visibly shivering, baby fur sprouting icicles.

At first she did not know what it was, ears flattened to its head, tail curled underneath. Then it blinked up at her and she saw that its eyes were an incredible opalescent blue.

It was a cat, a kitten cat. A halfway-grown creature, neither cat nor kitten. She did not like cats. She did not like the mystical way they looked at people. She emptied the rubbish into the dustbin and banged the lid. The rim of snow dulled the noise and the small cat barely flinched.

"Shoo," she said, but her voice was softened by the cottonwool flakes absorbing her breath.

She turned to go back indoors but tripped on an unseen edge and her slipper went flying. She hopped on one foot, her stockinged toes gingerly touching the icy paving stones. But the kitten cat had been lightning fast. He darted into the warm lining of the moccasin, trying to fold himself into a size five without success.

"Shoo," she said, exasperated, trying to shake

him out of her slipper but his claws clung like a limpet mine to the lambswool lining. She was getting wet. Snow was settling on her shoulders and the back of her neck. She picked up the slipper with the creature and hobbled indoors, a damp stain chilling the underside of her foot.

Once inside, the kitten cat jumped out of her slipper and shook himself all over the floor, creating a miniature snowstorm.

"Drat the thing," she said, putting her slipper to dry on top of the boiler. She did not like cats. She was not used to them.

The cat regarded her with a look of quiet acquiescence that said: I will go without protest if you turn me out but I will not fawn on you for hospitality. Strange how she could read that look. It was crystal clear in those amazing eyes. She poured herself a fresh cup of tea, and almost without thinking put a saucer of milk on the floor near the cat.

It sauntered over and sniffed cautiously. Its tongue darted out and the milk disappeared as the cat hardly took a breath from its lapping. Then it daintily mopped up the drops it had spattered and sat back to clean its milk-speckled muzzle.

It's starving, she thought with astonishment. The cat's condition was a shock. She had never imagined any such predicament. She did not want the responsibility. She wanted to be left alone in the cocoon of her empty house.

The kitten cat suddenly leaped six times its own height and landed gracefully on the boiler. It snuggled against her slipper, front paws

stretched out to dry, a small, enigmatic, unblinking sphinx.

"You're not staying, so don't make yourself
comfortable."

She went to the phone and dialed the local
police station. "I'm reporting a found cat, a
kitten."

"Is it a cat or a kitten, madam?"

"I simply don't know. Bigger than a kitten,
but not quite a cat. I found it in my garden.
Does it matter?"

"A young cat probably. About three or four
months old? That would make it a Christmas
present."

"I beg your pardon?"

"An unwanted Christmas present. They get
thrown out about this time of year, once the
novelty has worn off. Sounds abandoned."

She gripped the receiver. The words pierced
her. Her novelty had worn off too. She had not
quite come gift-wrapped with tinsel, but she
might as well have worn a label with his name.

"Where did you find it, madam?"

"By my dustbin."

She heard his patient sigh. "Address of same
dustbin, please. And description of cat in case
anyone inquires. There might be some distraught youngsters somewhere."

What did it look like? She had no idea. She
darted into the kitchen then came back to the
phone. "It's got peculiar darkish stripes on its
back and white everywhere else," she said, low-
ering her voice in a ridiculous manner. The cat

had fallen asleep on the boiler, one paw over its nose.

"A gray tabby," said the constable. "We'll let you know if anyone inquires."

"But I don't want it," she said, panicking. "Can't you take it away?"

"Sorry, madam, our cells are full. I'll give you the address of the local RSPCA."

She wrote it down on the back of an envelope. The desk had a pile of unopened mail. The branch was some distance away and it was too dark and too late to take it now. It would have to stay overnight.

Food. She had not cooked for days, eating only bread and jam, bread and cheese, bread and jam. She hardly thought a cat would eat a jam sandwich, however ravenous. She scavenged around in the top compartment of the fridge-freezer and found boil-in-the-bag cod in parsley sauce. It was a single portion but enough, surely, for a young cat and a woman with no appetite. She also heated some frozen peas.

The cat ate in straight furrows, vacuuming the plate several times till there was not a speck of sauce to be seen. It was dish-washer clean. She scraped her hardly touched fish on to its plate for seconds. The cat demolished it, then sat back to clean its whiskers fastidiously. It jumped on to the boiler and flaked out, small tummy distended.

"All right for you," she said, mashing the peas between two slices of bread. A minted garden-pea sandwich. She must be going mad.

Much later she heard a polite mew from the kitchen. The cat was hovering by the back door. Was it going? Did it want to leave, she wondered, as she opened the door. It leaped out on to an unhappy-looking flower bed and stood, poised, half expecting the door to be slammed.

"Well?" she grumbled. "I'm freezing."

It turned its back modestly and a moment later was kicking snow everywhere. It was a performance she had not witnessed before and she was bemused. Then with one bound it was back indoors, shaking snow off its paws.

That evening she actually stirred herself to do some sorting out. She went round the house and removed everything that had been his and the oddments he had given her. He had not been mean, only mean in spirit . . . he had not even shared his thoughts. She stored the stuff in carrier bags in the broom cupboard. The first Brownie that came to the door for jumble would get the lot.

She had forgotten the cat when she got up the next morning and nearly tripped over it as it lay stretched across her slippers.

"You're not staying," she said, putting her cold feet into the warmed-up lambswool. "And I've nothing for breakfast."

But she relented and broke a slice of bread into warmed milk. It was not critical of the sparse fare and ate with quiet gratitude. She rushed around, gulping cold coffee.

"Drat you, hurry up. I'm going to be late. You're going to make me late."

She pulled on boots, heavy overcoat, scarf,

and checked her keys. She did not bother with make-up these days.

A cold blast of air hit her unmoisturized cheeks and unprotected lips as she opened the front door and dropped the cat out. It landed four-pawed on a dusting of icy snow and shot her a desperate look. It was no good, she could not just go. She hurried back indoors, tipped shoe cleaners out of a cardboard box and picked up an unread newspaper. She cleared a patch of snow off the porch tiles with the edge of her boot, put the box on its side like a hutch with folded newspaper as a makeshift floor.

"That's all I'm doing," she panted. "Now I'm really late."

She hoped it wouldn't be there when she got home. She wanted it to go off somewhere, to leave her alone so that her mind need not be employed. But as she turned toward the house that evening, it was sitting like a sentinel on top of the box, tail curled neatly over its toes. It jumped down as she searched for her keys, tail held high, and shot indoors the moment the door was ajar.

"What a nerve," she said. She found a rusty tin of sardines at the back of the larder, which they shared. She made hers into a sandwich. That evening she went through her clothes and threw away anything he had particularly liked. It was very cathartic.

The next day she put adverts in local shop windows. FOUND: SMALL GRAY AND WHITE TABBY. It generated instant talk with the shop assistants. One gave her a leaflet on caring for kittens;

another gave her a sample of a new gourmet cat food.

The snow began melting into a dirty slush. A tidemark of wet crept up the cardboard box in the porch, and the top, where the cat sat, was sagging perilously.

"Why won't you go?" she despaired, renouncing the cat. When the box collapsed, it waited on the wall instead. Each evening it greeted her with a small, sweet mew of welcome as if it had been warned not to make too much noise.

No one phoned in answer to the adverts; she contacted the police again; she questioned her near neighbours; but no one had lost a small tabby.

"Dumped probably, from a passing car maybe," said one.

She searched for the RSPCA address but she had thrown all the mail away unopened. She did not know what to do. She could not phone the police station again. They would think she was a fool. Instead she bought six bunches of creamy-yellow daffodils; not one or two, but six. She filled three pottery jars with the blooms and stood them on the front windowsill like a declaration of independence.

For supper she cooked four chicken filets in a casserole with plenty of vegetables and baked potatoes. It would be enough for both of them, twice. She was washing up when the phone rang.

"Hello? Bette ... long time, no see." She laughed a little, smoothing back her straight hair with a wet hand. "I thought you were someone phoning about a cat. No, it would take too long to explain. Yes, I'm all right. Well, not all right but getting on somehow."

She paused while Bette's voice enthusiastically filled in the silence with words, an invitation to a club dinner.

"No, sorry, Bette. No more blind dates, please. One was enough. I know you are only being kind but I just don't fancy going out. I'm not ready for parties or meeting people. Scrabble?" She stopped and thought about small words. She knew cat. "I might cope with a game of Scrabble."

Bette hastily pinned her down to a day and time.

"I'll come round after I've made supper," she said. "Yes, thank you, a lift home afterwards would be nice. But I don't mind coming into the house on my own any more. You see, it isn't empty now."

She said goodbye to her friend and put down the receiver. She took her knitting out of a cupboard, a chunky sweater she had been making before he left, and turned on the television. There was a good play at nine o'clock.

The cat watched the preparations carefully and judged its moment. It had been waiting a long time, patiently. It jumped up on to the armchair beside her, squeezing down into the small gap at her side. It put one paw on her thigh to make sure she did not go away, the beginning of a purr vibrating in its throat.

She stared in surprise at the small creature, looking properly for the first time, marveling at the blotting-paper images of gray markings across its back. It was like seeing after being blind, a sunburst of delicate beauty that was stunning. She touched its head, amazed at the swansdown softness under her finger tips and the trust in the small furry face.

"Kitty," she said, getting the gender of the cat wrong. It was a natural mistake, not unlike her other, catastrophic mistake. How could she have known that the man she loved would eventually leave her, and not for another woman, but for a man? "I suppose I'll have to call you Kitty."

MALARKEY'S
MORTAL ENEMY

Malarkey's mortal enemy stalked him by day and by night. Stealthily it crept up upon him, rearing a dark, ugly head from side to side, always just that far out of reach, always just that much faster.

It was a constant threat to Malarkey's life. Not because Malarkey lacked courage. He would growl ferociously, darting in a fast bite to the enemy's most vulnerable spot, the throat. But the enemy bit back instantly and Malarkey was transfixed with agony, his amber eyes becoming pinpricks of pain. The black-faced creature had scored again.

Half the trouble was that the enemy had no eyes so there could be no eye-to-eye confrontation, no hissing and growling, no raised hackles.

Malarkey was convinced that he was larger than his foe, his eyes fiercer and more awesome, but he never had a chance to prove it. This made him very unhappy. He was not an aggressive cat in any other respect. He was affectionate and playful with his owner, a gentle retired schoolteacher called Miss Grayson.

Miss Grayson had acquired Malarkey to celebrate her retirement and the end of dismal journeys to and from school on the bus, staying late for study periods and teacher-parent meetings. It seemed a wonderful way to cement her independence and freedom. She had always wanted a cat but hesitated because of her long days at school.

Malarkey was a handsome mackerel tabby with clearly defined markings on his dense fur, narrow bracelets on his legs, necklaces on chest and neck and frown marks on his forehead forming an intricate letter M. It was this puzzled look that decided Miss Grayson.

"I know exactly how you feel," she said. "My own sentiments for years when faced with a classroom of reluctant scholars and a whole period to make interesting. Now, of course, I'm not sure what to do with the rest of my life. I'm in limbo. How shall I fill my time? I must do something."

Malarkey did not feel quite the same way. He had only one aim in life. He was already, even as a young cat, being plagued by the unseen presence of his sworn enemy. Sometimes it attacked him when he was asleep, a mean, cowardly trick, or crept up while he was quietly eating his supper. It even ambushed Malarkey on Miss Grayson's lap, an unforgivable act, sending the tabby yeoweling into a corner to lick his hurt pride.

"I'm glad I called you Malarkey," said Miss Grayson, straightening her rumpled skirt. "You certainly act in a nonsensical way at times. I can't think what's the matter with you. Come on out, you rascal."

Malarkey peered round the edge of the sofa to see if the coast was clear. He crawled out on all fours, eyes swiveling from side to side. There was nothing lurking behind the television set or under the coffee table.

He sat stiffly in front of the fireplace, momentarily disgusted that she did not know what was the matter with him, and Miss Grayson a teacher too. He wondered, not for the first time, if the enemy was solely in his imagination. Perhaps he had a few brain cells missing. Perhaps he had fallen on his head as a kitten, or been thrown out of a car on a motorway at an impressionable age just as a black container lorry roared by.

He was consoling himself with the lorry theory when suddenly the enemy attacked again. They fell into a bitter, biting battle, fangs snapping and crunching, fur flying.

Miss Grayson picked up tufts of fur from the carpet and wondered what she could do to help Malarkey. First she fixed a soft foam collar on him as protection. Malarkey took one look at the collar and went berserk. He tore at it with frenzied claws as the white rim kept him just out of reach of his foe. The enemy leered and taunted him. If it had had a face, it would have been laughing obscenely.

Miss Grayson withstood having a demented cat for half a day and then took the collar off him.

"I was only trying to help," she said, stroking down his ruffled fur. "I really don't know what to do with you."

Malarkey went into a contorted position for feline meditation. He tried to improve his ragged breathing. His physical level slowly came under control; he had to concentrate on his mental level. He needed a clear, relaxed mind.

The answer came to him in a flash. He knew what he had to do. He had to defend his home from this monstrous intruder. He knew now the purpose of this relentless onslaught on his person. He was being usurped in his own home. The enemy was simply waiting to seize power. Malarkey's eyes narrowed to slits as thoughts flickered, coming and going like silver minnows in the shallows.

An ambush. That was the answer. He must plan the most devious ambush in the entire history of the world, something so crafty and feline that only a cat could have thought of it. For once and for all, this black monster must be vanquished from the planet. The enormity of his solution staggered Malarkey. He prowled the floor, growling, making plans, refining strategies, the momentum of his wrath growing till he was walking on an impregnable high, his vision of conquest like a towering inferno.

"For heaven's sake, Malarkey!" said Miss Grayson. "Whatever has got into you this evening? Come and sit on my lap. We'll watch *Come Dancing*."

Malarkey's eyes glazed over with disbelief. *Come Dancing* . . . how could he concentrate on his master plan with all those little people swirling and twirling like mushrooms in the wind? He was mortified by her lack of sensitivity just when he was in his greatest creative mood. He sat on her knee with his back to her, the formation dancers mesmerizing him into stultifying boredom, trapped by her hand stroking his spine. A trap. Bait. A baited mouse. A mouse, a succulent mouse. He yawned widely. A maited bouse . . . he fell asleep, dreaming of swaying mushrooms.

"Good puss," Miss Grayson said softly, stroking his head in time to the music. She loved dancing but it was too late for her to dance now. Lots of things were too late.

The plan was fully formed when Malarkey awoke. Strategy: a succulent mouse (fresh) to be laid in a totally unexpected place. Therefore the garden was out. The front step was also out; the kitchen was out, despite its being the normal repository for food. Thumbs down also to the bathroom (all that nasty water). But how about Miss Grayson's bedroom? That might be perfect. Who would ever expect to find a mouse in that quiet, rose-sprigged room?

Malarkey became engrossed in the capture of the perfect bait. It took several days. His mortal enemy was also lying low, probably planning some absolutely barbaric counterattack. The mouse was found, tiny, brown, terrified. Malarkey knocked it cold with one quick swipe. He carried it upstairs on silent feet, his jaws careful not to mark it. He merged with the shadows, the taste in his mouth not of mouse but of victory.

He laid the mouse reverently on the carpet in front of Miss Grayson's dressing table, patting it into a natural position, then retreating to a hide-out behind a laundry basket.

Almost immediately his mortal enemy struck him a stinging blow across the nose. Malarkey saw stars. He leaped into the air, twisted, and sank his teeth into the mass of writhing black horror. The creature retaliated, fastening on to him with a punishing grip that made Malarkey's eyes water. He hardly heard Miss Grayson hurrying up the stairs and switching on the bedroom light.

Malarkey tried to wrench himself free. He caught sight of himself in the dressing-table mirror and froze. Was that him? That striped animal, jaws clamped on to a long black rope that was attached to his back, amber eyes flashing like beacons? The monster went limp, writhing away out of sight, wet fur flattened with saliva.

"Malarkey, you daft thing," said Miss Grayson, scooping him up. "Chasing your own tail again. When will you learn?"

At that moment she saw a twitching on the carpet as the bait (fresh) came out of shock. She shrieked and jumped on to the laundry basket.

Malarkey swung into action. He'd beaten his monster. Now that he knew what it was, he was no longer afraid. It was just a silly black tail. He'd got better things to do. The mouse scuttled under the bed.

"You get that mouse out of here," said Miss Grayson, finding her best classroom voice. "And I want it out of here before I come back. I hadn't made up my mind whether to go or not, but now I have definitely decided to go."

She grabbed her dancing shoes and fled. There was a ballroom dancing course at the local institute, starting that very evening. It said all ages were welcome. Anything would be better than staying in a house with a mouse. She might even discover the classes were fun.

Malarkey tapped his tail. The tufted tip flickered weakly. Malarkey's eyes blazed with satisfaction. He had beaten his mortal enemy.

THE
ICEBREAKER

Lesley had always been the shyest of people, right from girlhood. At parties she was dumbstruck; at school she was like a mouse; in the office they hardly knew she was there. Only the light clatter of keyboard confirmed that she had indeed arrived and was nose down into her work behind a forest of parlor plants.

Such extreme shyness came from a lack of confidence plus an inability to think of anything sensible to say. It was not that she disliked other people, quite the reverse. She wanted to talk. She longed to be part of the noisy throng, the gossipy groups, the party patter, but until she found something to say it was quite impossible to join in at any level.

It was on a delayed train journey home one

day that she discovered an interesting possibility. The train was motionless and driverless at platform nineteen in Victoria Station while a tannoyed voice crackled explanations about operational difficulties. Passengers began to talk, as they do in such situations. Lesley kept her head in her book. Each year she chose an author and studied his entire works. The Brontës had been fun, so had Trollope, but the Proust year had been hard going. Now she was reading Thomas Hardy.

"His name is Raffles," a clear voice came floating down the carriage. "Yes, because I won him in a raffle. It does seem awful, doesn't it, raffling a kitten. But since we were a group of cataholics, everyone longed to win him. He's a beauty ... see the pointed ears? A very good standard. And the little brick-red leather nose; another good point. You see, you have to look for these things if you intend to show."

The elderly lady enthralled an audience for fifteen minutes. Then the train started with a reluctant jerk and everyone retired behind newspapers or pretended to get the crossword right.

Later Lesley saw the woman alight, carrying a wicker basket with a lid. It was some days before Lesley found a similar basket. She wanted an enclosed basket that would allow air to circulate between strands of split wicker cane, but which restricted viewing. She did not want an open-style plastic wire cage.

She was amazed how fast it worked. She took

the basket to the office the next morning and set it down carefully under her desk.

"Hi, Lesley, what have you got there? Your picnic lunch?"

"No, it's ... it's ..." Lesley sought desperately for inspiration and her eyes focused on a headline in the morning newspaper: "OLD BAILEY JUDGE REBUKED."

"It's Bailey. Bill Bailey. Bailey for short." The words came out in a rush. She had not spoken so much for weeks.

"How interesting. Is it a puppy?"

"A kitten."

"Oh, what fun. Do let's see it, please."

Lesley froze, her tongue sticking to the roof of her mouth. She sought the newspaper again for help. "DAYLIGHT HOURS DEBATE IN HOUSE," she read.

"Can't. Daylight. He can't stand daylight. Something wrong with his eyes."

"Poor little thing. Will he grow out of it?"

"He might. Yes, he might. Definitely, he might."

All day she was visited by a stream of secretaries and messengers as the word went round. They thought it was rather sweet of Lesley to bring her kitten to work.

On her next visit to the library Lesley abandoned Hardy (temporarily) and took out several books on cat care. She was not quite sure what kind of cat Bailey was. Not an ordinary moggy, she felt sure.

"A Blue Birman," she told the next person

who asked her. "Very blue. Midnight blue. Extremely blueish."

"That sounds quite rare. Is he?"

"Oh yes, quite rare." At lunch times she took Bailey out for some park air. There were frequent offers of company.

"Sorry. I'm sure you'll understand. There are moments when a cat needs his privacy." And that, for Lesley, was such a long sentence that everyone understood immediately.

Even the cashier at the supermarket began to speak to Lesley instead of ringing up her modest purchases in glum silence.

"You're going to spoil that cat," said the cashier, pushing tins of salmon, sardines and tuna along the counter. "Start him off on Whiskas. Just as good."

"I want him to have the very best," said Lesley, forking out the money. "I think one's pets are worth it. Now, now, Bailey, stop scratching. You can't have your supper yet."

"Little rascal," grinned the cashier. "He knows it's for him."

"He's getting such a handful," said Lesley. "He climbed up the curtains last night."

"You'll have to train him. Can't let him wreck your place."

Lesley began a course of training for Bailey. The office was fascinated by the details. At first she concentrated on simple obedience commands. *No* was the key word.

"No," she said firmly to Bailey through the wicker. "Stop chewing your basket. You've had your breakfast. No, you can't come out. Remember your poor eyes. No, Bailey. No, stop that at once."

"What's he doing now?" they asked, peering between the slats into the inner gloom. They thought they saw a vague shape, a glint of bright eyes.

"He's being very naughty," said Lesley mysteriously. "And I won't allow it. Even a cat has got to obey a certain code of conduct."

In a short space of weeks, Lesley progressed from having friends: nil, to having friends: masses. It was exciting. Everyone spoke to her, in the library, in the street, at bus stops, on the train. Even those who did not speak walked past with an indulgent smile at her obvious devotion to a cat. It made life very pleasant.

The only discord began in the park one lunch time. She took Bailey with her for his customary airing and change of view, eating her sandwiches as she sat watching the ducks gliding on the pond, occasionally slipping Bailey a flake of tuna or sliver of cheese. She was admiring the blue sheen of the neck feathers on the ducks when a man spoke to her.

"You shouldn't feed a cat bread," he said. He was also eating sandwiches.

"I am not feeding my cat bread," Lesley bridled. "I simply gave him a little fish."

"Why don't you let him out? I've seen you before at lunch times. You never let him out. Poor thing, stuffed in a basket all day. It's cruel. You could train him to go on a lead. Cats are perfectly trainable if you start them young enough."

No one had ever rounded on Lesley so vehemently. She was quite taken aback. "I'm not being cruel to Bailey," she managed to say.

"I'm wondering if you are a fit person to be in charge of an animal," the man went on. "It's a very small basket to be cooped up in all day with no chance of any exercise."

"It's a very small cat," said Lesley. "And I'm wondering if you've ever been told to mind your own business."

The man, thirtyish with tidy brown hair, looked surprised. Lesley was also surprised by her fluency and courage, but both commodities were deserting her fast. She threw the rest of her sandwiches to the ducks and hurried back to the office.

"I may not be able to bring Bailey to the office every day now," she announced to her colleagues at tea break. "He's growing. He needs to run about . . . in a darkened room."

"Oh Lesley, you must bring him! Bailey is our mascot. We'd miss him. Besides, he'd be lonely all day in your flat without us to talk to him."

"That's true." And she would be lonely without Bailey to talk about. Without Bill Bailey as an icebreaker, she would be back in her silent, wordless world. Still, there was Bailey's increasing size to worry about.

It kept her preoccupied, and she did not recognize the new accountant behind the desk when she took an urgent print-out up to the Accounts Department.

"What are you doing here?" he asked. He looked different with dark-rimmed glasses perched on his nose. His eyes were fixed on her face and Lesley felt a swift pang of desolation. The name plate on his desk said *John Parker*.

"I—work here." She managed to bring out three words without Bailey's help.

"Where's your cat?"

"Under my desk." Another three words.

"Let's go out tomorrow lunch time and buy a cat collar and lead and see if we can get your cat used to it. The reception area is usually deserted at that time. We could try some practice runs, a few minutes at a time. Don't worry, he won't be able to escape into the street. My mother breeds cats. I'm quite used to them."

It was all too much. Lesley fled. Her computer skills went out of the window and she nearly erased a valuable file. She gave so many contradictory instructions that *Error in Document* kept popping on to her screen. She omitted to keep an eye on the residual bytes and had to abandon a whole piece of work when she overran.

Severely shaken, she hurried home, not taking her usual pleasure in the comments that Bill Bailey generated.

"Your little cat is very good," said the vicar, smiling benignly.

"He sleeps a lot." She peeped through the wicker, trying to keep her voice steady. "He's asleep now, one little paw over his nose."

Lesley slept badly that night, disturbed by dreams about cats that grew as big as elephants overruning the reception area. When she awoke, she was in no fit state for a dreadful journey.

British Rail had decided that morning to pull out all the stops. There were operational difficulties: staff shortages, a train derailed, a signal failure, leaves on the line, a minor maintenance strike and the computerized ticket machine was on the blink.

Lesley's train eventually arrived late, only three carriages long. It was standing room only. After finding a space to plant her feet, she put the cat basket on the luggage rack. The train shunted up the line a few stations, then terminated without notice and everyone had to get out, cross under a subway and wait for another train to complete the journey.

She struggled through the subway with the seething mass of disgruntled and irate passengers, completely disoriented. It was only as she saw the empty train shuttle off to some depot that she realized what she had done. She was speechless with distress. Every word she had ever uttered left her. She ran back along the platform, waving her arms helplessly.

"Cat," she gasped.

"Go across to platform one, lady," said a porter.

"Bailey," she choked.

"Old Bailey? You'll be wanting London Bridge then. You can get a bus from there."

Somehow Lesley got to the office. Her stricken face said everything. Her friends crowded round, offering sympathy, coffee, to share her work load.

"But where's Bailey? Is he ill?"

"Lost," she croaked, back to single words.

"Lost? But where? How?"

"Train."

Slowly they dragged the story out of her. She wept into a mug of coffee. John Parker appeared and took charge of the rescue operation.

"Have you phoned Lost Property or informed the railway authorities? I'll check at the station first. Someone may have handed him in. What about the Transport Police? They could intercept the train before it gets taken to the repair yards."

"John Parker, you're so bossy," she stormed at him through her tears.

"And you're irresponsible," he shouted back. "If you don't do something fast, there'll be a dead cat in that basket."

Lesley ran weeping into the cloakroom while everyone rounded on John Parker for being unfeeling and callous. Bill Bailey had become so real and so much a part of Lesley's life, she could not imagine how she would survive without him. He was her prop, her stay, her reliable companion and friend, and she missed him desperately.

The rail service miraculously returned to near normal the next morning. Lesley opened a book but could not read a single page. She tried to think calmly. The solution was to buy another basket and pretend that Bailey had been handed in at Waterloo's Lost Property office and some kind person had looked after him overnight. Her spirits revived at this simple explanation.

She would have to go out and buy an identical basket without delay.

As she walked into the office, she wondered why there was a crowd round her desk, laughing and talking all at once. They moved aside as she approached.

"Bailey's been found!" they told her, practically cheering. "Isn't it wonderful! John went and fetched him first thing this morning. And he seems perfectly all right, and his eyes have got better, and he's absolutely adorable!"

The five-months-old Blue Birman looked at her from inside the safety of John Parker's jacket. Its clear baby-blue eyes regarded her with curiosity and a tinge of apprehension. The accountant walked toward her and carefully put the young cat into her stunned hold.

"This is Bailey," he said, his spectacles hiding the degree of knowing care in his eyes. "I found him for you."

"My Bill Bailey?" she repeated, all resistance melting as the soft little bundle crawled into the comfort of her arms.

"Don't you recognize your own cat? But I'm afraid your basket's a goner," he added. "Damaged in transit." He did not mention the pile of cat-care books he had found inside.

"I was going to get him a bigger one anyway," she said fluently. "The kind with an open end so that he can see out."

"Bailey will like that. And a lead?"

"And a collar and lead."

"I'll phone my mother. She'll know just the shop," he said, briefly touching her hand as she stroked her very own cat. "We'll go at lunch time."

RADIO ALLEY

Good morning, folks! This is Radio Alley on the air, bright and early, this sunny Thursday morning. The weather forecast predicts a temperature of 23°C by mid-day, followed by low cloud in late afternoon and scattered showers by the evening. But stay tuned, this is cheery, cheeky Alley Cat, your dawn DJ, bringing you the music of your choice, what you like, when you want it. Pin back your ears, folks, here comes Michael Jackson in 'Bad, Bad, Bad'!"

Al went into his routine. He could do a brilliant Michael Jackson, even if he said so himself. But it was exhausting. The voice was dead right but the jerky dance steps were hard on four feet. Michael Jackson did not have to perform intricate choreography on the three-inch-wide top of a brick wall. It was the only place from which Al could reach his vast audience.

Al stopped in his tracks. A late request was coming through . . . for Sarah Brightman singing her show-stopping aria from the *Phantom of the Opera*. It was a bit out of his range.

"Sorry, Madge from number fourteen. I do understand that this is the first anniversary of your torrid affair with that Don Juan at flat seven, but I'm right out of time. Try again next week, Madge . . . and Happy Anniversary!"

Al slunk round to the back doorstep and waited, pretending he had been there all night, cold and lonely. She let him in eventually and he was torpedoed into a pink dressing gown for his good-morning smother.

"Darling Alley Cat. What a naughty pussy. You didn't come in when you were called. Out all night again. I ought to give you a whack."

Al forced through a quick purr to pacify her then leaped out of her arms to head the queue at the refrigerator. These mysterious whacks. She was always going to give him a whack. He was not sure what they were. Some kind of gift for the good and virtuous, perhaps? Both attributes were somewhat beyond him. He was a born alley cat, rescued by the kind Lilian Jones from a precarious life of scavenging and fights and near starvation. They lived in a back-to-back house in an old part of Newcastle, almost in the shadow of the great cathedral with its rare crown spire.

Lilian existed for her radio. It was on all day, and her life was dominated by the programs;

the volume was rarely touched. She worked at home, putting braid on lampshades—latticed, bobbled, straight, wavy—her output accompanied from early light by Derek Jameson, through Ken Bruce to Jimmy Young, *Woman's Hour, The Archers, A Book at Bedtime;* and sometimes, when she was busy with a rush order, into *Round Midnight.*

It was no wonder that Al became a radio freak.

Lilian was a good worker. These were no chain-store lampshades but exclusive specials made for luxury yachts and hotels and Arab palaces. She worked with the best silk. She was given a design to follow for each batch. Her nimble fingers sewed and glued, not a speck of dust ever appearing on the hand-made silk or expensive parchment.

Al respected her work. He knew it had close connections with his menu, and a cheerful "Haddock this week, Alley," sent shivers of anticipation along his elegant spine.

Though Alley was a rescued cat and had one torn ear, he had grown into an extremely handsome long-haired midnight-black tom. All the females around the streets were crazy about him and it was partly this disconcerting and uncontrollable adoration that channeled his talents into radio. He made it quite clear from the beginning that nobody, but nobody, got a request played if they hassled him.

"This is the nine o'clock news," announced Lilian's radio.

Al rushed out into the tiny garden and leaped

to the top of the brick wall via an ancient and dusty coal bunker and a stack of wood.

"This is the nine o'clock news, folk," he bawled in a loud, penetrating voice. "Last night, Gorgeous Gussie got thrown out of the Old Bull again. This is the third time in a week and steps are being taken. The kittens at number four are finally weaned and homes are being sought. Miss Lilian Jones is currently working on gold-trimmed bedside lamps for the refurbishment of a luxury hotel in Marrakesh."

Al paused. He had absolutely no idea what that last news item meant but it gave the bulletin a certain class. "Mrs. Parker's parrot, Nosey, has died of overeating. Amen. The goldfish at number eleven have gone down the loo. Any sightings should be notified to the distraught owner. A moment's silence, please, for our dear, departed friends," he added smugly. He had always hated the parrot and the goldfish were particularly wet.

"Back at one, folks, for the next up-to-date bulletin. This is Alley Cat, Newcastle-on-Tyne, signing off for *News at Nine*."

Returning at his leisure to the kitchen, he lapped up a saucer of milk to ease his microphone throat and fell fast asleep. It was an exhausting business, running a radio station single-handed. In his dreams he heard the cooker being lit, the scrape of a dish, then an appetizing aroma of fish wafted around his nostrils.

He streaked into the garden, tail high. "News flash! News flash! Poached haddock for lunch!"

The daily *Archers* was a doddle. Al had a long, rambling serial going about a family that was always discovering lost sons and daughters, rowing with interfering neighbors, dynasties founding and crumbling, characters being shot and coming to life again. It was all very confusing and sometimes Al did not know where he was in a story line. He usually brought in some startling new development so that his listeners also lost track. No one ever complained.

Woman's Hour was more of a headache. Worthy subjects did not come easily to mind. To spay or not to spay had been done many times and his female audience were decidedly anti; the value of homoeopathy for cats had limited interest; consumer tests on dry food always resulted in begging letters; the age-old dilemma of in or out at night had been flogged to death. He was hard put to find new topics.

By the time he reached *A Book at Bedtime*, he barely had the strength to haul himself up on to the wall. His *Prayer at Midnight* was usually a series of high-pitched amens which reverberated along the empty streets and had people throwing up windows and chucking old paperbacks at him. His listeners loved the prayers, though. They joined in all the amens with great feeling and released emotion.

"Closing down now, folks," he yawned hugely. "See ya in the morning. G'night."

"Will you so-and-so cats shut up? I'm trying to get my sleep," a male voice cursed.

Al pushed open the door and slipped quietly indoors so the poor man could get his sleep and also so as not to wake Lilian. She never locked up. Nothing worth pinching here, she always said.

He was normally a careful cat, treading his way delicately between Lilian's materials, never snagging a fringe or upsetting her workbox. But that night he was particularly tired. He did not see the precariously balanced pile of ivory drum lampshades looming in the dark like the Tower of Pisa. Suddenly the tower toppled, enveloping Al in a cage of wire, cutting off sight, sound, movement. He panicked. It was so unexpected. He fought fiercely, tossing lampshades round the room in all directions, shaking off the one perched rakishly on his head. He retired trembling and indignant to a dark corner, licking down his fur.

Lilian was understandably annoyed in the morning, having to tidy up before she could begin work. "And the van's coming at nine o'clock. I'll be hard put to have this lot packed by then."

Al sat grooming his whiskers. It was nothing to do with him. He refused to acknowledge any responsibility, but it would make a good news item. "Monster tower crushes intrepid reporter . . ." the fluid phrases came effortlessly to mind.

"Well, at least there's no damage," said Lilian, going into a fast stacking routine. She put the shades quickly into the boxes provided, hardly looking at them.

A few days later, Al had just come back from a particularly spectacular commentary on a feral fight near the river, when he found Lilian crying over a letter.

"They're docking all my last week's pay," she said, trembling. "Work not up to standard. Shades dirty inside, they say. Covered in coal dust, they say. But that's impossible. I was very careful. They've scrapped the whole batch and sent them back. I don't believe it. I'm always so particular."

Al could not look Lilian in the face. Coal dust. He slunk away, tail down. He knew where the coal dust had come from. He closed down the radio station for the day. Operational difficulties, he announced in a choked voice. He couldn't even bring himself to play funeral music.

A whole week's pay. Lilian certainly could not afford to lose so much money; nor could he. Bread and milk were acceptable if she had temporarily run out of tins, but not as a staple diet. He was going to be hungry and Lilian's spotless reputation was now besmirched. That hurt even more.

The situation triggered a remembrance. Al racked his brains to pin it down. The key was somewhere in his past, something so far off in the mists of time that it shifted in and out of his mind like an elusive shadow.

Radio Alley went on the air again the next morning.

"Business as usual," Al announced. "Sorry for the hiccup, folks. In order to celebrate the relaunch of Radio Alley, we are holding a grand competition with magnificent prizes, repeat magnificent prizes. The puzzle is: What is long, noisy and has oranges rolling in the gutter? Answers please before sundown. The first prize is ..." His gaze wavered halfway between the grimy chimneys across the road and the woman next door putting out the refuse bins. A prize ... what could he offer that could be in any way construed as a prize? He had nothing. He did not own anything. Then he saw his long beautiful black fur, as dark as midnight, glistening and rippling. He had nothing to offer but himself.

"First prize will be an intimate supper for two at Miss Lilian Jones's house. No expense spared!"

That ought to do it, he thought. That ought to help him identify an elusive memory.

All day long the listeners arrived with their entries for the competition. They dropped by the wall in droves.

"I've never seen so many cats," said Lilian, looking out of her window. "Shoo, shoo ... go away."

The guesses ranged from an express train in a tunnel to a stolen salami sausage; from the dachshund at posh number five to Mr. Parker coming home drunk from the Old Bull.

Little Madge appeared. She was a slim and dainty gray tabby with wide and appealing blue eyes. She had gone off Don Juan completely in the last few weeks, and the competition had given her something different to think about.

"Is it a street market, Al?" she suggested timidly. "Cloth Market or Market Street? Perhaps the Cattle Market, somewhere round there?

Newcastle has so many markets. It's not far from here. I'll show you if you like, oranges and all."

That was it. Al remembered it all now. He remembered the days and nights when he was a lost kitten wandering the street markets, trying to find food among the oranges in the gutters, kicked by feet, drenched by rain, miserable and forlorn, waiting to die.

It was quite a problem steering Lilian Jones in the direction of the street market. Between them, Madge and Al managed it by getting under her feet and playing hide-and-seek and making complete fools of themselves. They did not know that she had been going to the market anyway, to find cheap food, to buy bruised bargains at the end of the day. She was desperately short of money.

But Lilian was not a complete fool. When she saw the noisy, bustling market with its multitude of stalls, the variety of seconds and secondhand goods on sale, she knew what she could do. She asked around, arranging to share a stall the following weekend.

She came home triumphantly, late on the Saturday evening, scooping Al up into the folds of her double-knit jersey. "I sold them all, Alley. All those lampshades! They went like hot cakes. I couldn't believe it. All that quality stuff, just a little bit of coal dust inside, which nobody minded. I made more money than the amount they docked from my pay. Think of all those luxury shades being put on Newcastle bedside lamps tonight. It was so exciting. But I've brought home some nice liver for your supper tonight. I'm sorry about all the bread and milk recently. Forgive me, Alley Cat."

Al rushed out into the garden and bounded up on to the wall even though it was starting to rain. He was ecstatic. He had saved Lilian. "News flash! News flash! The budget statement from the House is that financial ruin has been averted. Liver for supper. And now the result of the Radio Alley competition. The prizewinner is the delightful Madge from number fourteen. Well done, Madge. Congratulations."

Madge slid out from the shadows and curled round the washing post.

"What about my prize?" she purred. "That intimate supper for two?"

"Did I say that?" Al played for time.

Madge blinked away the rain. "And I have won."

"I'd be honored . . ." gulped Al, for once at a loss for words. He could only look at the length of her eyelashes, drown himself in the fathomless blue of her eyes, wonder at the crystal tips of rain on her fur. She was so small and beautiful.

"You said magnificent prizes," said Madge shyly. "You did say magnificent, Al."

Al swallowed hard. "I'll think of something special," he said, knowing he was lost.

SKINFLINT

The man was so mean he thought it sensible to put a lock on the refrigerator door. The telephone could only be used by prior notice and each call was strictly timed, entered in a notebook and a charge calculated.

He also charged his wife for produce grown in the garden plus a suitable mark-up for his toil and sweat. It was a wonder he did not charge for his services in bed but, since he was inept and boring, Edith reckoned she deserved a discount.

In their courtship days, Edith had thought Godfrey a thrifty and careful provider. When he split the bill for their honeymoon, she should have paid her half and taken flight there and then. But it was too late. She was already pregnant with their first child, a boy. Two more boys followed quickly and Edith became imprisoned by the house and her maternal instincts and the relentless labor of bringing up a family.

Godfrey's meanness took on new proportions. He scrutinized her weekly accounts, checking the receipts; chiding her for each two-pence-off coupon that was not used by the correct date. He dictated when the children should have new clothes; the boys had to sign for their meager pocket-money allowance even before they could write. Edith did not get any. If she wanted a lipstick or some tights, she had to pretend that the till receipt was a special soap offer and bluff it out.

By the time the boys reached their teens, Godfrey had installed electric meters in their bedrooms, worked out a time-and-motion study for the household chores and decided that Edith had time to do a part-time job.

"But I don't want to go out to work," Edith protested. "I've more than enough to do looking after the four of you. Besides, after all these years, there's nothing I'm capable of doing."

She wanted to add that she was tired, too, and worn out with living with Godfrey. But it was not a word that Godfrey understood. He had been blessed with excellent health and could work non-stop in the garden until the light faded and he could hardly see what he was doing. It saved on electricity.

"What have you got all these lights on for?" he'd growl, stomping through the house and switching off the surplus. "One light each. No one should need more."

Edith was darning. She needed a brighter light on the dark socks. She put down the wool and stared at the wall. The television set had no plug. Godfrey only put the plug on at the weekend when he wanted to watch sport.

"There, I can see you've got nothing to do," said Godfrey. "Just twiddling your thumbs, wasting your time as usual. I'll make out a new time-table for you to follow."

"Why don't you fine me for wasting time?" Edith suggested. "Or install a toll machine outside the sitting-room door? How about a levy on unproductive or negative conversation?"

Godfrey looked at her blankly.

"I could pay you in blood. Then you could sell it to the blood bank. What a wonderful way to make money. I'd soon be reduced to a skeleton and you'd save on clothes, food, heating, everything."

Godfrey ignored her ramblings and made a series of calculations on paper. "You've got at least four hours a day which are unproductive. I'll find you a job."

"And a cat," said Edith swiftly.

"What? A cat?" Godfrey repeated the word as if it was a foreign language.

"That's right. If I've got to go out to work then I've got to have a cat, too. I've always wanted a cat, and as the boys start to leave home I shall be lonely." Their eldest son had already moved to a bedsit in Clapham.

"But a cat is a totally useless creature. It eats

and drinks and contributes absolutely nothing to the household. No, definitely no."

"It might catch mice."

"It might catch rain."

"No cat, no work," said Edith with more determination than she had felt for years.

"Vet bills."

"I'll pay for them from my wages."

Godfrey could see that Edith was quite adamant about having a cat. Every time he brought up the subject of work, she immediately produced a list of facts that supported the therapeutic value of a cat.

"All right, all right, you can have your damned cat!" he shouted, grudgingly. By now, getting Edith out to work had become an obsession. "But a free one, mind. Nothing fancy. There's a job going filling shelves at a supermarket in town. Discount for staff purchases. You'll be able to get dented tins for the cat. Drop a few, know what I mean?" he added, making the first joke of their marriage.

Godfrey did not keep his word about getting Edith a cat. There were always excuses about not being able to go to the rescue center. He became absorbed in the problem of how to get her wages, which were paid weekly in a small brown envelope. Eventually he gave up, but instead deducted the amount of her wages from the housekeeping. Edith had already managed to keep two wage packets to herself before he hit on that idea. It was wealth beyond all her dreams. She hid them in a shoebox.

"You won't need housekeeping now you're

earning," he said, putting his money back in his purse. "Your pay'll do us two nicely when the boys have all gone."

"I haven't got my cat yet," said Edith.

"Your cat! Your cat! That's all I hear from you. Can't you say anything else?"

"Yes. When are you going to get it?"

Godfrey strode out angrily and Edith stopped mentioning it. She put in a few hours' overtime and kept quiet, hiding away the extra money. One day she set out to find the rescue center. It was quite a long journey, involving a change of buses.

"Sorry," said the supervisor of the cats' home. "We haven't got any kittens at all. It's the wrong time of year. Come back again or give us a ring."

"I'd really like a kitten now," said Edith. "I've traveled a long way. It might be difficult to come again."

"How about an adult cat? We get a lot of homeless adult cats. It's sad. Either the owners have had to move, or found they can't cope. Sometimes an old person dies and there's no one willing to take on the cat."

"I really wanted a kitten," said Edith uncertainly.

"Just have a look at them," said the supervisor, who was a good judge of character. "You might change your mind."

Edith changed her mind immediately. As soon as she saw the grown cats, thoughts of a kitten vanished. Rows of eloquent eyes gazed at her, some pleading for a home, others full of a gentle dignity that touched her heart.

"What a beauty," she murmured as a fluffy white Persian rubbed at her hand with a soft head. "Fancy leaving a cat like this. It's beautiful."

"Owners dumped it here while they went on holiday. Never came back. Needs a lot of grooming, that one."

Edith felt her own hunger for a cat growing. She wanted them all. She could not make up her mind.

The last cage was empty. Edith was about to turn away when a slight shift of gray shadow caught the corner of her eye. She peered into the gloom.

"That's Ragbag. A very nervous elderly cat. We'll never find him a home, not even if a fortune went with him. He's unplaceable."

Ragbag moved stiffly on arthritic legs. He was almost ugly, with a thin bony face and sharp pointed ears; his speckled gray tabby coat was short and sparse; his eyes were watery.

"Poor old thing," said the supervisor. "Nobody wants him."

"I want him," said Edith suddenly, recognizing a kinship.

She took Ragbag home in a cardboard box with some ointment for his eyes and some vitamin pills for his arthritis. She knew how he felt. She was unwanted too, except as a provider of meals, sock-mender, son-bearer, filler of shelves.

Godfrey was not at home when she got in. She opened the lid of the carrier. Ragbag refused to get out but crouched nervously in a corner. She lifted out a stiff, resisting body and tried to hold him, but he struggled free, ran berserk round the room then squeezed himself behind the sofa, almost out of sight.

She crawled about on her knees but all she could see was a dark shape in the furthermost corner.

"You stay there for a bit then," Edith advised. "Till you get used to me. I daresay it might be difficult with Godfrey at first, seeing as how he's not exactly in favor of having you here."

It was several days before Ragbag found enough courage to emerge. Edith continued feeding Ragbag behind the sofa, and he made the odd dash for the litter tray. Then he peered out, long nose sniffing and exploring. He sniffed her hand and tentatively she gave him a little rub behind the ears. Memory cells awoke in his mind. He stretched his neck towards her.

"There, there . . ." she said, very quietly. "Not so frightened now, eh? Look what I've got for you today. A nice tin of sardines. They'll put a shine on your coat."

Ragbag crept out toward the enticing fishy smell. It was a long time since he'd had sardines—back in the halcyon days of youth, running and leaping after pieces of string and bunches of dried grass. Oh, those carefree days, where had they gone? How had he got inside these old bones?

When Godfrey saw Ragbag for the first time, his eyes popped wide. "What an ugly brute. You could at least have got a proper-looking cat. I'm not wasting money on that. Take it back."

"Been left a fortune, that cat has," said Edith. "Didn't you read it in the papers? 'Cat Heir to Thousands from Widow Recluse.' "

Godfrey did not know whether to believe her or not. Edith had been behaving very oddly lately. The cat stared at him from the safety of Edith's arms. The cat did have a certain air about it, a certain shabby dignity.

"Rubbish," he said, but he wasn't sure. He counted the tins of cat food in the cupboard, checked off new purchases against his current food inventory. Everything tallied. Even the level of the opened tin in the refrigerator was right.

"Half a tin a day. No more, no less."

"Half a tin a day," Edith agreed, not stipulating tin of what. Salmon, tuna and sardine were on Ragbag's additional vitamin-filled menu.

Gradually, as the sons left home, so Ragbag blossomed. The more he moved about and played with Edith, the less his arthritis seemed to trouble him. He was intelligent and invented games for himself, like pretending the clothes horse was an igloo or a cave or a wigwam, and repelling invaders from behind the curtain of washing.

He sat in the wash basin, catching drips from the tap; that was a waterfall game. He played peek-a-boo through the banisters; another jungle game. He tunneled under the eiderdown, chasing monsters from the bed; such fun, a battle of the giants. He jumped into her shopping basket, and when Edith had thrown a tea towel or duster over him, he would keep very still and pretend that no one could see him.

"I can see your tail!" she would say, giving it a tweak.

Oh, they were days of fun and laughter. Edith began to look younger, happier.

"You are the funniest cat," Edith laughed as she chased him under the eiderdown. "But I must make the bed, or I'll be late for work."

Ragbag's contribution to life made Edith realize how laughterless and spiritless the years before had been. The quality of his coat improved to a rich sheen though the bony face stayed the same; he was still the ugliest cat in town. But he was friendly and outgoing; that is, to everyone except Godfrey.

When Godfrey appeared, Ragbag hid behind the sofa, under the bed or at the back of the linen cupboard. He knew his days were numbered if Godfrey had his way. Godfrey's meanness escalated to unbelievable extremes; he canceled the newspaper, rationed tea bags, aspirins were counted, all envelopes reused, old cards recirculated, bath foam banished, coffee abolished. Edith even had to grow her hair to save on having it trimmed.

"But Godfrey . . . my hair looks awful," she wailed, tucking the long ends out of sight.

"Cut it yourself. Nothing to it. I do it all the time."

Ragbag hid under the sofa. He was convinced that Godfrey was mad. When Godfrey found Edith's new building society account book, the man's crumbling control snapped. It was only a modest account, saved from her overtime, but Godfrey went to pieces.

He raged, he threw things, he tore the account book into shreds. Edith cowered, white-faced, hands gripping the edge of the kitchen sink. She was terrified, but part of her wondered why she had put up with Godfrey for so long. She could not stay, not now. Godfrey was shredding the only part of her that had been truly hers. She would go to one of her sons. She would take Ragbag in his cardboard carrier.

"You deceitful woman," Godfrey boiled, his face going red. "Hiding money away behind my back. A secret account. Where did you get it from, I'd like to know? Was it payments from this recluse, this widow?"

"I worked," she said faintly. "I only worked, as I always have."

"Well, you're not working there any more if this is what you do with it. We'll get you some piece work to do at home where I can keep an eye on you. I'll supervise what you do and what you earn. If your earnings are down, we'll have to economize, and the first thing to go will be that damned cat!"

Edith hardly listened any more though Godfrey stormed on and raged at her for a good twenty minutes. She would have to go; there was no doubt about that. She had no choice. But how did one leave? She could not even begin to think how to go about it.

"I'll get rid of that cat right now," Godfrey roared, having worked himself up into a monumental fury. He pulled the sofa out from against the wall. Ragbag shot between Godfrey's feet with a brilliant turn of speed for an old 'un and fled upstairs. Godfrey charged after him. Edith heard Godfrey's curses as he cannoned into furniture, slammed doors, his heavy footsteps stumbling from room to room.

Edith couldn't move. She could not think what to do. Ragbag raced into the kitchen, panting, chest heaving as the years caught up with him, his amber eyes staring with panic. Her shopping basket lay on the floor. He leaped into it and in a flash she covered him with a kitchen towel.

"Where's he gone?" Godfrey hollered from the doorway.

"Out of the door," she said.

He cursed loudly and stomped out into the darkening garden, falling over the dustbin, which he had put outside the door to check through. He came in, clutching his foot. "I'll get him in the morning when he comes in for his breakfast." Godfrey's hands trembled as he got a screwdriver to put the plug back on the television set.

"I'm going to watch the telly," he said. "I'm upset."

Edith swept up the shredded paper of her building society book and put the bits carefully into an old envelope. Godfrey was sprawled in a chair, asleep in front of the flickering screen.

She put on her coat, scarf and gloves, fetched her handbag and picked up the basket with Ragbag curled up inside. She let herself out of the house without a backward glance. She would walk to her eldest son's place. It would only take about an hour and she was used to walking. He would let them both stay until she found a place of her own.

"We'll be all right, you'll see," she said to Ragbag, giving his bony head a reassuring stroke under the kitchen towel. "I've still got my job. I can earn enough to look after both of us. Why, I might even get another cat, company for you while I'm at work. We'll see if that white one is still there. It's time we both came out from behind the sofa," she added.

Godfrey could not believe that Edith had gone. He wandered round the empty house, muttering to himself.

"She'll be back. She'll be back. She can't manage without me. Never has, never will."

He did not bother to clear up, clean up or wash up. That was Edith's job. He left the chaos of the cat's flight strewn all over the house.

It was a pity he also left Edith's newly purchased can of hair spray where it had fallen off the dressing table and rolled across the carpet. She had bought it in an effort to tame back those long ends while she was at the supermarket.

The next day it lay in a patch of strong sunlight as the temperature rose to the mid-eighties. At 1:36 P.M., the hairspray canister exploded and set fire to the carpet, and in minutes the house was burning. Godfrey hurried home, stunned. Of course, he had never taken out an insurance policy on the house or its contents. Insurance was a sheer waste of money.

He sat among the smoking rubble, looking at his locked and blackened refrigerator and feeling hungry. He couldn't even find the key.

OTTER
SPOTTER

They stared at each other for fully half an hour. The cat was pure white underneath with pale gingery tabby markings on her back, head and tail. All four legs were white; her mask was white and her whiskers long and lustrous, her eyes deep as a forest pool. She was undoubtedly beautiful; a creature of medieval fairy tales and supernatural powers.

The otter was a mess. He sat upright on a log, his dark coat pointed and spiky with mud and water; his head fur flattened to his skull; his monkey-like claws clinging to the bark of the log, nails long and uncouth. His black nose twitched, and his dark berry-bright eyes were intent on surveying this strange visitor. He had never seen a cat before.

Samantha had never seen an otter before. She was equally amazed. She had seen horses and dogs and shuffling hedgehogs since they moved out to the country, but never an otter. Her name was Samantha because her family thought she was very Page Three. It did not mean she was misshapen or over-endowed, but her whole image was glamorous and a bit unreal. Since they never shortened her name to Sam, she did not mind too much. She had a loving home, and if they occasionally laughed when introducing her to friends, she accepted that sometimes humans had a weird sense of humor.

It was almost *Beauty and the Beast* all over again, this meeting of otter and cat. Samantha knew she was beautiful. Otter knew he was a big, clumsy, wet, hunted, ugly-faced wild creature. What could they have in common?

Staring at each other had one solid result. No attack was imminent. Samantha's claws retracted. She lifted one damp paw daintily from the wet undergrowth and shook it. Otter shook his whole body vigorously and spray hit the overhanging trees.

Samantha would have retreated. She did not like getting wet but the otter intrigued her. She had never seen an animal so big and fierce, and yet instinct told her he was gentle at heart. Being a cat of infinite curiosity, she wanted to find out. So she waited and watched.

The wood had become a great adventure. Her family lived on a new housing estate at the edge of the wood, and people did not venture too far into the dense trees. It looked too alien for town folk. Nature rambles and picnics and innocent playing among the bluebell dells were things of the past. The wood was shunned.

This was fortunate for the otters. There was a good running stream and no one troubled them. The otter-hunters did not even know there were otters around.

The otter's boredom threshold was low. He pushed a stone over the ground, watching the cat's reaction. There was none beyond the merest twitch of a pale fluffy tail. He rolled over on to his back with his current favorite toy, a pine cone. He juggled it expertly in his paws with gleeful enthusiasm and exuberance of spirits. He could juggle for hours without dropping the cone.

The cat yawned with exquisite elegance. She was impressed but she was not going to let this tubby clown-like creature know. Samantha could sit for hours without moving.

The otter rolled off his back and squirmed in the mud, then he shot off, his short legs taking him with agility to the top of a sandy slope. Fearlessly he launched himself down the toboggan run, landing at the bottom with a squeak of triumph, romping around among the moss and marsh marigolds, full of play and energy.

It was a delight that almost communicated itself to the cat. But Samantha was not ready for any relationship with such an odd creature. She stretched herself into a graceful arch and stalked off home, leaving the otter merrily tobogganing by himself.

But she was soon drawn back to the woods,

following a path toward the stream that ran between high banks covered in undergrowth. There were hundreds of leafy tunnels and alleys among the undergrowth and she slipped along them as silently as a fawn shadow. She saw the prints of broad, capable webbed feet in the mud and knew the otter was not far away.

This time he was in the water, shooting like an arrow after trout, chasing eels with a forward diving roll. He was so fast and yet on the surface he swam with a clumsy doggy paddle. Suddenly he caught sight of the cat and came bounding up the bank as if they were old friends, shaking water off his fur in all directions.

Samantha retreated in horror. She leaped up on to the low branch of a willow tree and regarded him with disdain.

But there was no end to the otter's good nature. He gamboled about and then went to find one of his hidden treasures. He came back with an empty Coke can with which he had devised a deadly game. It required split-second timing. He sent the can rolling and skidding down the toboggan slope, then threw himself after it, deftly catching the can before it could disappear into the undergrowth. Samantha grudgingly admired his turn of speed and skilled fielding. Her whiskers trembled. She longed to pat the clattering red and silver can. She longed to launch it on its dizzying plunge down the slippery slope.

Otter paused for breath. He was at a loss how to amuse this pale fluffy thing now perched up a tree and pretending to be a bird. He racked his brain, fussing round the tin, wondering which of his treasures would appeal. He had some nice flower heads, a cigarette packet, shells and stones of all shapes and sizes that had taken his fancy. He chittered and chirped, trying to coax Samantha down from the tree, but she refused.

Eventually he gave up and dived back into the stream as fast as lightning, cavorting and tumbling under the water with all the grace of an acrobatic dancer.

Samantha sat still in the tree, riding out her disappointment at his departure. It was her own fault. She had wanted to play. She just did not know how to begin.

The house where Samantha lived had a child. This child played all the time. Its favorite game was throwing everything out of the pram for someone else to pick up. Samantha knew what she was waiting for. The moment the child threw out a soft orange and green ball, Samantha darted forward and caught it in her mouth. In a flash, she was off down the woods, her prize clamped in her jaws.

The cat deposited the ball carefully by the bank and withdrew a few yards. The otter's eyes lit up with delight. He saw endless possibilities in the bright globe. He patted the ball tentatively along the ground to judge its weight and durability. He tossed it into the air, catching and tossing. Then he rolled on to his back, juggling with all four paws in wild joyousness.

Quite deliberately he sent the ball flying in Samantha's direction. Before she realized what she was doing, she was chasing after it, her beautiful tail streaming in the wind. She pounced on the ball, growling, tossed it around, shook it, batted it back to the otter. The other chittered and squealed ecstatically.

He inventively devised new games. The ball was given the toboggan-run treatment, dropped from the bank on to the stepping stones, sent skimming across the water's surface. Soon the sodden lump bore no resemblance to the neat Mothercare plaything thrown carelessly out of its pram by the child.

Samantha went home exhausted and ravenous. Otter had not offered her one of his eels, but then she would not have known how to eat it if he had.

They played all summer. A variety of articles disappeared from Samantha's house. She was seen dragging a large empty cardboard box into the woods. The otter laid it to waste in one glorious afternoon of rampage and destruction, bits flying in all directions. He loved all the new things Samantha brought him. Once it was a terry nappy which had fallen off the washing line. He rushed around waving it like a banner, snapping and whipping the towel with flourishes in true matador style.

Sometimes Samantha played, sometimes she just sat and watched. She grew more adventurous in his environment, crossing the stream on the stepping stones, trying a little fishing from a precarious perch on the bank. If it rained she curled up in the dry hollowed-out tree stump where the otter slept.

She slept through most of a heavy rainstorm and did not realize how much earth had been washed off the bank. Otter was totally unperturbed by the storm, only half aware that the level of the stream had risen and a lot of debris was being washed down in the muddy water.

Samantha went to greet him as he bounded out of the water, not noticing that the surface of the bank had changed. She was taken by surprise, slithering and slipping as her claws tried to find a hold in the mud and loose soil. Her frantic clawings were useless. She tumbled backwards into the swirling brown water, gasping, the current dragging her midstream.

Otter sat bolt upright on a fallen branch, vast whiskers quivering, eyes alert. He saw that his playmate could not swim and squeaked with alarm. He plunged into the water, pulling along the fallen branch, his sharp teeth clamped on to the bough.

The cat was wallowing round in dizzy circles, neck deep in water, paddling fiercely in some attempt at self-preservation. Otter pushed the timber into her path and her claws clutched at a fragile hold. He dived below and surfaced under the panic-stricken creature, heaving her up with his strong, muscular back. Somehow she scrambled on to the branch, water streaming off her dirty white coat, eyes stuck with mud and water. Otter pushed the load toward the bank. It touched land momentarily with a shudder, paused, the swollen current already tugging it away.

Samantha jumped. She landed on a clump of reed, then clawed herself frantically to higher, firmer ground. She crouched, shaking and panting, then was very sick. When she felt less weak, she crept back home and did not stir from the warmth of the house for days.

Otter thought he had lost his friend, but she came back. Their playing took on a new dimension. Samantha matured and became less concerned with her dignity and appearance. Otter took her further into the wood and showed her his special places and delights. There was a hidden waterfall and a dam, a great fallen oak, an island of tangled undergrowth.

Autumn came and the first night frosts curled the edges of the summer leaves. The bracken was turning and a sharpness in the air reminded the otter that he had to prepare for the winter.

One day men came to the edge of the woods, parked a van and unloaded a pile of equipment. Samantha watched from the safety of a fence. She did not like the look of the bundle of netting. The men were joking and laughing, enjoying themselves. They divided the equipment between them and began to tramp through the woods, quiet now, not talking. Samantha followed them, a shadow they never saw.

The men found the prints of the otter and discussed this find among themselves in low voices. Samantha did not show herself. She knew the otter's habits. He would come bounding out of the water to greet her, not knowing the men were there.

Suddenly the otter appeared from a different direction, a new treasure tucked under an arm. He stopped, alerted by the odd scent of men, uncertain, not yet alarmed. He lived such an innocent, carefree life, danger was not really known to him.

The men tensed. Samantha saw the net rising in the air. With a high, screeching yowl, she leaped on to the shoulders of the nearest man, sinking her claws into the flesh of his neck. He dropped the net with a shout of pain, stumbled and fell, trying to dislodge whatever had attacked him.

Otter took one long distraught look at the struggling men, and then at Samantha, turned and plunged into the water, diving deep down as fast as lightning, swimming with desperation and courage towards the estuary and the rough sea. He did not know where he would be safe. He swam for miles until he was exhausted.

Samantha still sits and waits patiently in the dense wood. Sometimes she rolls a pine cone down the overgrown toboggan run. One day the otter will return. Perhaps in the spring.

THE RICHEST CAT IN THE WORLD

"**H**ow much?"

Mr. Sinclair, the solicitor, read out the figure again. He faltered over the sum. There were so many noughts.

"All for a cat! I don't believe it. Aunt Lenora must have been off her rocker."

Fiona sat back in the chair, biting her nails. "It's hardly fair. Think of the number of times we've had her to lunch."

"Every Christmas. Every Christmas we had her to lunch," said her nephew Tom morosely.

"And the presents we gave her."

"A plant every birthday," Tom added.

"And she leaves everything to a damned cat! Thousands and thousands of pounds. Can we contest the will?"

Mr. Sinclair cleared his throat. He thought

the niece and nephew might ask that question. It was an unusual will, but then if he had any money he would be unwilling to leave it to such a grasping pair. Lenora Finch had not been blind to their avarice though she'd had little idea of her own worth in those last years.

"No, it's all neatly sewn up and perfectly legal. The money is invested in a trust fund of which I am one of three trustees. You and your husband are the legal guardians of . . . Darkie." He hesitated over the name. It seemed daft to be talking about a cat, even a nice sedate-looking cat like Darkie. "The money is to be spent making the rest of his life happy and comfortable."

"Why can't he go into a commercial cattery?" Fiona asked petulantly. "It would be so much simpler."

"Miss Finch specifically wanted Darkie to live out his remaining years in a normal home environment."

"And when he dies?" Fiona asked hopefully.

"What's left of the trust fund goes straight to several animal charities."

Fiona flung herself back in the chair with a groan. "Well, that's that then," she said, glaring at her husband as if it was his fault. "We shall have to look after the damned cat."

Darkie sat on the windowsill, keeping still and quiet. It had been a strange few days and now this argument in Lenora's sitting room, with no one taking any notice of him, was even stranger.

Lenora had talked to him all the time. They

had talked about everything under the sun. She had not minded if he sat on top of the newspaper while she was poring over the financial pages, or curled on her lap while she was on the phone to Mr. Sinclair.

"I've got Darkie on my lap so he'll bring me luck," she always said, stroking his thick black fur. "Buy the shares, Mr. Sinclair!" Darkie had often butted her chin in agreement; it was really his way of telling her how much he cared and that luck had nothing to do with it.

He knew that Lenora was ill when she took to her bed. She told no one at first. It was a struggle for her to get up and find him some food. He provided his own, a few mice, bread from neighboring bird-tables, water from puddles, but Lenora still tried to open tins with her arthritic fingers. He lay on her bed at night, listening to her wheezing, a sadness curling round his heart like icicles.

He was there when she died. He stayed for a while to make sure, but he knew it was only a shell in Lenora's form and that his dear friend had gone. He padded round the house, sitting in dark corners, wondering what would happen next.

For several days he coped on his own. None of the neighbors remembered that Lenora had a cat, so nobody looked for him. People came and went. He had been forgotten. Darkie sat around politely, waiting to be told what to do.

Then the noisy couple arrived. He knew them, all right. They had come occasionally to see their aunt, bringing her cheap plants that promptly withered. The young woman had a loud, piercing voice that affected Darkie's sensitive hearing.

"She must have left it to us," said Fiona, valuing the pictures. "After all, we are her only relatives and she owes us something. We were very good to her really, coming to see her and everything."

"I wouldn't call twice a year being very good," said Tom. "We did the barest minimum. The usual thing one does for old, unmarried, unwanted aunts."

"Nonsense," said Fiona. "Here comes Mr. Sinclair at last, with a briefcase. That's encouraging. For heaven's sake, look more cheerful, Tom. You look as if you're going to a funeral."

"We have just been to one."

Darkie did not understand what followed, except for hearing loud shrieks from Fiona and grunts from Tom. He heard his own name mentioned, but did not let on that he recognized the word. It would not do to appear too intelligent in the circumstances. He did not trust the noisy couple.

"He's a very nice cat," said Mr. Sinclair, closing his briefcase. "I'm sure he'll be no trouble."

Fiona had been thinking fast. "The trust fund is there for all expenses incurred in looking after Darkie. Have I got that right?"

"That is correct."

"We live in a flat on the fourth floor of a block in central London, hardly suitable for a cat. If we bought a house with a garden, I presume that would be an expense incurred on behalf of Darkie?"

"I presume so."

"Food—the very best available—and all vet's bills?"

"Of course."

"Then I should need a car to take him to the vet. One could hardly expect such a valuable animal to travel by bus. Monthly check-ups at the vet's would be imperative. After all, we both want Darkie to live a very long and happy life, don't we, Tom?"

Tom took his gaze away from the window and the unkempt flower beds. He preferred living in a flat. He did not want a garden, but his wife's eyes were already glazed with house-hunting and choosing the curtains.

Darkie's whiskers drooped. He liked this old Victorian house with its polished wood paneling, dark spidery corners and furniture that smelt of apples and almonds.

"What about this house?" Mr. Sinclair suggested. "It's quite roomy."

Fiona laughed hollowly. "Heavens, what a dreadful idea. It's a mausoleum, a museum. It gives me the creeps. I like new houses, everything modern and bright."

"I prefer flats, somewhere central," said Tom, but no one was listening to him.

Fiona bought a large new house on an exclusive private housing estate. It cost a whole row of noughts from Darkie's inheritance. It was modern and spacious enough, thought Darkie, as he explored his new home, room after room with long, elegant windows looking out on to a sculptured garden. He was willing to settle down here, but it was strange how so many things were called "not allowed."

If he jumped on a velvet chair, Fiona shrieked: "That's not allowed." If he kneaded a duvet, she pushed him off, saying: "That's not allowed." The coffee table was out of bounds, so were the counters in the clinical kitchen. There were so few places left to him. Apparently windowsills were all right if he did not eat the plants; most floors, but certainly not the pristine pale Chinese carpet. No one knew he had discovered the back of Tom's wardrobe. Darkie perched among a heap of old trainers which Tom was loath to throw away and tried to sleep, remembering the grass-tall summery and sparkling cold wintery days with Aunt Lenora when he had been allowed out.

For he was not allowed out now at all, never, ever. Fiona forbade it, despite having a garden for him. He was too precious, too valuable, too rich, whatever that meant. He had to use a litter tray, which he hated and kicked all over the floor when she wasn't looking. He could only watch the outside world from inside, chasing mice and stalking birds in his imagination, sniffing at windowpanes to recapture the scent of sappy leaves and bonfires. The house smelt of deodorants, air fresheners, expensive perfumes. His nose could isolate the chemicals from the natural musk and flower oils. He could track down a synthetic in five seconds. It was the nearest he got to hunting, these days.

He was well fed. He could not complain about the cuisine. Fiona bought prime steak, turbot, chicken livers, free-range turkeys, scampi, lobster. It was not necessarily for him. Most of it was their food but Darkie got the bits, the trimmings, the left-overs. Fiona was extravagant, so he did well.

"But don't give him the cream," she snapped at the new maid. "We don't want Darkie to get heart trouble."

The only time Darkie went out was for his monthly check-ups at the vet's. There was a pale blue Rolls in the garage for such visits. It was very comfortable, except he was not allowed to explore. He had to stay in a closed traveling basket.

The vet gave him vitamin injections, patted him on the head and said he was in tip-top condition. Then they drove back to the big house and Fiona parked the Rolls next to the Mercedes she used for shopping.

Otherwise, Darkie lived in the shadows, moving silently from one patch of concealment to another. He rarely miaowed. Fiona didn't like him making a noise. She said his wailing gave her a headache so he learned to keep quiet. Sometimes he miaowed hopefully at the utility-room door, but no one let him out.

"I think we ought to have a swimming pool," said Fiona, forking up dainty mouthfuls of shrimp cocktail. Darkie slid under the table in case a delicate morsel slipped off her fork as she waved it in the air.

"I don't see how you can possibly justify the

cost of a swimming pool to Mr. Sinclair. He was very dubious about the last lot of bills. Cats can't swim."

"Cats don't play billiards but you managed to get an extension built on for a table."

"I admit I had to talk old Sinclair into it, but when he heard that Darkie liked chasing the balls . . ."

"But now he's not allowed to!" said Fiona triumphantly. "In case he ruins that precious baize."

"How about your cruise to the Caribbean? What have you told Mr. Sinclair about that, eh?"

"That I'm exhausted, of course," said Fiona, the fork suddenly too heavy to hold. "Looking after Darkie is a twenty-four-hour job. Night and day. I hardly take my eyes off him. And you'd better sharpen up while I'm away; no staying out to all hours with your cronies. The cat will be your responsibility and you'd better do the job properly."

"Don't you worry," said Tom, his voice stiff with sarcasm. "I'll look after our little gold mine. It's only a cat, after all."

Darkie stayed as still as a sphinx. A few crumbs of Stilton came his way. He darted forward like a phantom, his pink tongue licking up the morsels with deadly accuracy.

"Perhaps we ought to buy him a cage," said Fiona thoughtfully. "One of those big show pens. Then we'd be sure that Darkie was safe all the time, and I could go away knowing you won't make any stupid mistakes."

The pen arrived by special delivery. It was

designed for showing champion winners at cat shows, very white, very modern, with a sleeping area and fitted litter tray. Darkie looked at it in alarm. Before he knew what was happening, Fiona was carrying him at arm's length and depositing him in the cage. The hatch door slammed down. Solitary confinement had begun.

"Now he'll be safe," she said, snapping the catch.

Darkie explored his prison. It took a whole minute, even looking at everything twice. He was too well fed to squeeze between the bars. The hatch was rigid. He patted the catch but the spring was strong and impregnable.

Fiona went off on her cruise in a flurry of shrill goodbyes, the boot of the Rolls packed with matching sets of new Gucci leather luggage.

"No racing, no drinking, no going to the theater. Watch the video and the cat. Remember, he's our bread and butter," she instructed.

"And jam and cream and caviar and vodka," added Tom under his breath. "Not to mention an extravagant wardrobe of clothes and enough perfume to scupper a U-boat."

Darkie perked up his ears. He remembered racing in the garden . . . chasing leaves, mice and moles, shadows and the wind. Perhaps Tom would take him along to the races. He'd like that. Tom might even like it. He never sounded particularly happy. Fiona had made him give up his job in the City, and he was a disheveled heap of male frustration.

Tom looked after Darkie for a couple of days, then the draw of the racetrack was too much. He was bored and Fiona would never know. He left the maid to feed Darkie and clean out the litter tray. Darkie watched her carefully. She was a simple girl and he only had to wait for her to make a careless mistake.

"Drat it," she said to herself one afternoon, the litter tray half in and half out of the cage. "I need a new bag of that litter stuff. Stay there, pussy, while I go and get it."

Darkie did not stay one second longer than it needed for the maid to go out of the door to the store room. He leaped over the tray and through the open hatch. He raced into the hall and up the grand staircase. There must be a window open somewhere. His nose followed a current of fresh air. A bathroom window was open . . . He leaped up, knocked over shaving equipment and aftershave lotion, and stood poised for freedom on the sill. A sloping roof was within jumping distance. He made a wild leap on to the tiles, scampered along the ridge, skirted chimneypots and aerials, slid down to a lower level, and then with a final bound he was free in the garden.

He was thrilled. He ran and danced, leaping at leaves, boxing butterflies, his fur streaming like dark silk. He had a glorious afternoon, chased a magpie but forgot to bow respectfully; climbed trees, listening to the soul music hidden in the vibration of their branches.

Exhausted, he curled up in a sunny spot and let the warmth of the afternoon lull him into a contented sleep.

Suddenly he was struggling in mid-air, paws like windmills, claws unsheathed.

"Thank God, I've found you! You bad, bad cat. Getting out like that. I'll kill that girl."

A large masculine hand thumped his rear. Darkie looked at Tom in shock. No one had ever hit him before. His thick fur was good insulation but his dignity was hurt.

"Running away, were you? I'll see you don't run away again. I'll make sure of that."

Darkie hardly thought that lying asleep in full view on the patio was running away, but how could he argue? He was carried indoors like a parcel and tipped into the cage. He heard the prison door clang shut. A big steel padlock appeared.

"Get out of that, Houdini," said Tom with some satisfaction.

The padlock was cold and heavy, not user friendly. Darkie peered through the bars at his jailor but Tom was busy pouring himself a Scotch on the rocks and did not see the cat's shattered look. The ice clanked in the glass, like a dozen padlocks.

Darkie crawled under the blanket provided for him, hoping the darkness would make the nightmare go away. What was the use of being the richest cat in the world if he did not have his freedom? This existence was pointless. He would rather be living in the poorest house, with the poorest family, managing on scraps and earning his keep by holding the mice at bay.

He growled at a bit of blanket that was tickling his nose, just to keep his spirits up. He had to do something to protest about the current state of affairs. But what could one small black cat do? And who would listen, anyway?

It was one of the maid's less memorable suppers. She had been instructed to put ready-made frozen dinners into the microwave for Tom, but she did not really understand the timing, The incinerated chicken pieces thudded into Darkie's bowl. Tom slammed the door as he went out to get a meal at the local pub.

Darkie sniffed at the offering. Charcoal was not his favorite dish. He was not hungry, in any case.

He was not hungry the next day either. His milk had gone sour and he hated fish heads. He knew the maid had taken home his fillet of haddock and substituted the fish heads. He didn't blame her. He doubted if Fiona paid a decent wage.

Not eating made Darkie feel a little light-headed. By the end of the week he was floating. No one noticed; the maid was unobservant and Tom was out all the time. It was left to Fiona to discover that their gold mine had slimmed down to skin and bones.

She arrived back from the cruise, golden brown all over, with several extra bags of souvenirs, sarongs and Barbados rum. She tripped indoors, flinging her fur wrap down on the chaise longue, shedding inflight magazines and chocolate wrappers all over the place.

"Tom, Tom darling," she called. "Where are you? I'm home! Your Fiona's home!"

She roamed the rooms, calling her husband. There was no answer. Tom had gone out. He was investing some of Darkie's fortune on a horse called Puss in Boots running in the three-thirty. It needed his personal attention.

"Well, that's wonderful," she stormed. "I come home at last and there's nobody here to greet me."

It was some hours before Fiona had finished unpacking and wandered into the kitchen. When she saw Darkie, she was staggered; her pale blue eyes widened with fright. He was so thin, the knobs of his spine prominent, his once beautiful dark fur dull and lifeless.

She shook the maid. "My God! What have you done to the cat? Haven't you been feeding him?" she screamed.

"Yes, ma'am, of course I have, ma'am. I've been putting food down and clearing it away. A clean plate every meal, just as you told me, ma'am."

"But has Darkie been eating it? I left a mountain of steaks and coley and liver in the deep freeze for him."

The maid paled, remembering where all that good food had gone. "I don't know, ma'am. I really don't know."

Fiona did not wait for Tom to return. She carried Darkie out to the Rolls in his traveling basket and drove to the vet's. Her hands were trembling on the steering wheel as she exceeded the speed limit, and the big car took the sharp turns without slowing down.

She made such a fuss in the waiting room

that the vet saw her straight away. He slid his hands expertly over Darkie's emaciated body, looked in his mouth, listened to his heart and lungs.

"Malnutrition," he said, noting her tan disapprovingly. "Been on holiday, have you? Just left your pet to fend for himself?"

"No, I did not!" she protested indignantly. "There was the maid and my husband to look after him. Darkie gets the best of care and attention."

"But obviously not this time," said the vet, stroking the bony skull. "We'd better keep him in for a few days. He needs a fluid intake, vitamin injections and a high-protein diet."

"I don't care what it costs," said Fiona, panicking. "Just keep him alive."

Darkie's new quarters were interesting. Plain but warm and functional. He was too weak to go far but he could see that he had a run outside with a real tree in it, and there was a way for him to go in and out as he pleased. A pretty kennel maid came and coaxed him with some minced chicken baby-food. He ate a few mouthfuls, just to please her, his eye on the tree. It was still there. No one had taken it away. He could almost feel the texture of the bark under his claws.

She poured out some warm milk and tickled his ears gently. "A few sips, Darkie. Come and try some . . ."

His health improved in days and before long he was in and out of his quarters, leaping up the tree and hissing at his neighbors just to enliven things. They hissed back and everyone had a good time.

Mr. Sinclair drove along the private drive to the new house. Tom and Fiona had certainly done well for themselves. The house was imposing, with four white pillars at the entrance, the lawns greenly manicured, their gleaming cars parked in the circular courtyard. It seemed far too big for two people.

"Oh, Mr. Sinclair," Fiona gushed from the chaise longue on the patio. "We weren't expecting you. How nice. Would you like some tea? I'll ring for the maid."

"No, thank you. No tea." Mr. Sinclair came straight to the point. "It's about Darkie. I've come to tell you that your guardianship has been terminated. Unknown to you I have been receiving monthly reports from the veterinary surgeon, and the last report was most disquieting. Your lack of concern for the cat's welfare is quite shocking. Darkie was found to be half his normal weight and could only have lasted a few more days. I and the other trustees have decided that you are no longer suitable people to be caring for a dumb and helpless creature."

"But that's not true. It was all a terrible mistake," Fiona floundered. "We've always done everything for Darkie. Look at all the lovely things we've bought him."

"The terms of the will were for a loving and caring home environment," said Mr. Sinclair. "He was on the point of starvation when you returned from your holiday cruise. That's hardly a caring attitude."

"It was that stupid maid!" Fiona whimpered. "Don't take Darkie from us."

"I shall be making other arrangements for his care. You may keep the house and the cars as recognition of your services, but no further bills will be honored."

Tom did not contribute a word. He knew what he wanted to do. His old job was still open, and he'd soon find a suitable flat. Puss in Boots had come in at five to one and that would help. Fiona could stay on in this huge house visiting her posh new cruise friends till the hospitality ran out.

Mr. Sinclair collected Darkie from the vet's surgery. He blamed himself for not being more involved in Darkie's welfare, but some tricky litigation had been taking all his attention.

He had brought along an old traveling carrier from Lenora's house. It was made of much-chewed wicker and was open-fronted, so Darkie could look out and around. Darkie recognized it and jumped in without being told, turning round and settling down, fur quivering, his nose twitching against the crossed bars. It was his box, his very own, the one Lenora had used.

"Now, how are you feeling, Darkie?" said Mr. Sinclair, reversing slowly so that the carrier was not unduly jolted. "Better, I hope. I'm afraid you are still going to have to take a few extra vitamins until you are in tip-top condition, but you won't mind that, will you?"

Darkie regarded Mr. Sinclair with surprise. He had never really looked at the solicitor before. He was a small, slim man in his middle fifties, with receding hair but warm brown eyes that spoke to him with affection.

And there were more surprises. They drew up outside Aunt Lenora's old house. Darkie could hardly believe it. Had living with Fiona and Tom been a dream, a nightmare? Had he never been the richest cat in the world? Was he just an ordinary cat again?

"I bought Miss Finch's house last month," said Mr. Sinclair, searching for his key. "I've always rather liked it and it suits an old bachelor like me. There have been a few changes, of course, but not many. You'll find it pretty much the same. Come along in, Darkie."

Darkie raced round the house, upstairs and downstairs, sniffing old haunts, the carpets, the windowsills, the chairs. He was ecstatic. Only Lenora was missing.

"And come and look at this, Darkie," said Mr. Sinclair, leading the cat to the back door. "I've had a cat flap fitted so you can go in and out as you please. You'll soon get the hang of it."

Darkie's heart filled with joy. One glance and he had got the hang of it. He longed to bound out and see if the garden was the same, but he contained his excitement for a few moments longer, in order to purr his gratitude round Mr. Sinclair's neat, navy-clad ankles.

Then he pushed purposefully through the cat flap and surveyed the unkempt garden with wonder. A few extra weeds, a few new cheeky tits, but he and Mr. Sinclair would soon get it into shape.

Mr. Sinclair watched with amusement as the

cat inspected the garden. Lenora's house suddenly felt right. He would enjoy coming home
and finding Darkie here to welcome him. He
knew they were going to become very good
friends.

As he prepared their evening meals, Mr. Sinclair thought about the lie he had told Fiona.
He had not been receiving monthly reports from
the veterinary surgeon. He had only paid the
bills as and when presented.

Even now he didn't know if he had been
dreaming or in that strange no-man's-land
when emerging from a deep sleep. But he had
heard Lenora's voice quite clearly. "Call the vet,
Mr. Sinclair," he had heard her say in the same
commanding way that she had ordered him to
buy stocks and shares. "Call the vet."

So he had.

THE TOOTING BEC COWBOY

I rode into town on 9 July, a day when the midsummer sun rose over the street litter bins like a prairie fire. It was hot. I was hot. The whole town was about to explode.

Coming in on the tailboard of a container lorry was not my normal way of riding in. I preferred something more flamboyant to suit my lifestyle, but there were some real bad hombres around this territory and I didn't want them to be alerted before I was ready to pin them to a wall.

If they knew I was coming they'd hold the high cards, and I was dealing them no trumps.

It reminded me of the last time the wire tapped out an urgent message for me. An old homestead in Lime Street had been overrun with rats and the locals couldn't cope. When a tabby granddaddy died of a wound that went bad on him, the wires started humming and they sent for me.

I had those rats running scared in less time than it takes to spit out a herring bone. I walked ten feet tall. My reputation spread like a parched desert swallowing rain.

"That cowboy, that Tooting Bec cowboy! Now he's really something and a half," they said in all the late-night dives. "If there's trouble, that's where you'll find him."

I headed west but the wire was tapping again. I got the message and I didn't like the sound of it. A pack of ferals, real bad bandits, had taken over a building site, terrorizing the peace-loving inhabitants of the locality, waylaying, ambushing, stealing from their homes till they were afraid to go out at night.

"Tooting Bec! You gotta come and help us! We need yer. These bandits gotta be taught a lesson."

So I rode in early before the town woke. I wanted to find my own stake-out without causing a ripple. I carried no weapon. Everyone knew that. I hate to kill but I love justice. And justice was what I was out to get.

A row of old shops and offices had been demolished to make way for a multi-story car park; then the money ran out. This was the site, derelict, abandoned, reeking a sour odor. The demolishers had left behind piles of rubble, old portacabins, rusting machinery. The locals were ditching trash, sagging mattresses, broken armchairs, a pram with crooked spokes. The ferals moved in and made it badlands.

Warily, I left the container lorry and, taking advantage of the traffic, eased myself along below a hoarding. I had to find myself somewhere to rest up and take stock of the situation. There was no way any old garbage can would do for me. I had style. I had class. I could speak Mexican.

"Mama mia, just looka dis cat! It's bigga danna dawg!"

Mama Mia scooped me up into her plump arms and marched me indoors. "We keep," she said, plonking me down on a counter. I hissed madly, showing my strong white fangs. No one messes around with me.

"And so fierce," she beamed. "Good for mice. No mice, clean shoppa."

The smell of chilli and tomato bean sauce wafted across my nostrils. There's nothing I go for more than meatballs and pasta in a garlicky sauce. There were dishes and bowls on display. They smelt good. It was an Italian delicatessen. Italian or Mexican, what did it matter? Italian was near enough. I could take or leave the chilli con carne. It was tagliatelle carbonara from now on.

I leaped up on to a top shelf and reconnoitred the display of tins. At the far end I squeezed into a space ten inches by fourteen inches. From it I got a clear view of the demolition site. This was my stake-out. I would stay.

"He maka dis his home already," said Mama

Mia, clapping her hands. "I maka da special dish for him. Pescatore, with clams."

I spent the afternoon surveying the ferals. They were a sly lot, creeping around and disappearing so I couldn't get their number. The leader was a big black cat, brown at the edges. He had a mean face. I called him Bruno.

That night I went to the nearest dive in a disused church cellar. It was as still as a grave. No one was having any fun. The crowd looked at me with apprehension; not a whisker twitched. I loitered in the doorway. If anyone made a wrong move, I was ready.

A worried-looking tabby got up and hobbled over to me. He had an infected paw and it hurt him bad.

"Well, if it isn't Tooting Bec! We're mighty glad to see you, cowboy. You're just what this town needs."

"I heard you were having some trouble," I growled.

"Look what they did to me," said the tabby, holding up a deep bite.

"It's real rough, Tooting," said Kitty, a sweet young tortoiseshell with innocent baby-blue eyes. "I haven't been able to visit my auntie for a whole week. We're afraid to go out at nights."

"Get your things, Kitty," I said, flexing my muscles. "I'll take ya to see your auntie."

I never avoided trouble. I wanted to force a showdown with Bruno. It would save me the hassle of hunting him out.

"Let's go, sweetheart," I said, pushing over the door.

The night was pitch black. We walked down the street together, Kitty trotting primly by my side. I knew we were being watched. We had to cross the road by the demolition site. I saw a dark shadow creep out of the yard. I could smell the skunk. It was Bruno.

"Thinking of crossing the road, stranger?" he snarled, slitted green eyes glistening with evil intent. "Ever thought what it's like to be squashed by a bus, my pretty one?"

Kitty shrieked, her speckled fur trembling with fear. She closed in by my side, standing her ground.

"You ain't nobody, you dirty old feral," she spat.

"I ain't dirty and I ain't old," he growled. "I could run you round the block and still have time to trim your whiskers."

"That ain't no way to talk to a lady," I drawled dangerously, arching my back, my fur standing on end. I could look big, real big, and just as mean. There was fifteen pounds of hard muscle packed round my body and I was ready to spring. My claws were blade-sharp; my fangs strong and deadly. A low rumble of fury began to generate in my throat.

He took a second look at me, hard-eyed with suspicion. The other ferals were lying quiet. He backed off, crouching, tail whipping the dust.

"See you around, stranger," he hissed, furtively watching my every move.

"Nobody gets in my way, scabface," I warned.

I shared my supper with Kitty. She ate dainty like a lady and Mama Mia was enchanted, but my mind wasn't on the clams or Kitty. Bruno and I had got to have a shoot-out. It was either him or me and it wasn't going to be me. It was a mean trick, but when the chips are down you gotta have bait, and Kitty sure was bait, baby. It was walking on a slippery sidewalk but I figured I could handle it.

I took her home and left her in the porch.

"You were really brave tonight, Tooting," she purred.

"Think nothing of it," I said, sauntering off into the moonlight.

Don't take me wrong, I was no hero. I had never toted a badge but I knew how to put my head down on a tricky situation.

The shelf at Mama Mia's was hard and cramped but my bones had never known a soft pad. I bedded down without a sound. Around me lay the dark shadows of the shop, the ghostly gleam of washed counter, the wide valley of wall between mirrors. I knew Bad Bruno was spoiling for a fight. He nursed an evil hatred for everybody and everything in sight. I eased my long frame out on the shelf and tipped my tail over my eyes.

I caught a few mice for Mama Mia the next day to pay my due and was rewarded with blistering hugs. I didn't tell her I got them from the graveyard at dawn.

"See how he clean uppa for me?" she glowed, all sweaty.

That was me, Mr. Clean. But how did she know? I scrutinized her through narrowed eyes, wary. Did she know something I didn't know?

I had to make sure. I had to know if Mama Mia was with us or against us. I became aware of every detail, the tomato stain on a cloth, the empty vinegar bottle on the floor, the spreading wet ring from a defrosting chicken. She wasn't gonna catch me out.

I found Kitty asleep on the tin roof of a hot saloon. It was an old jalopy, registration J. I climbed up beside her, frying my paws. She yawned a pretty pale pink cavern of a mouth, showing the furled pink velvet of her tongue.

"What do you know about Mama Mia and Bruno?" I asked, straight to the point. "Does she feed him and the rest of the outlaws?"

"Good heavens, never," said Kitty, claws retracting. "She hates them as much as we do. They steal from her dustbins and leave a mess. Once they stole a whole chicken from her kitchen."

"Thanks," I said, jumping down. "That's all I wanted to know."

"Ain't yer staying?" she asked, peering over the roof with wide blue eyes.

"I got things on my mind," I said, stalking off, cold sober. "I'm riding out."

"Don't leave us, Tooting," she pleaded, but I didn't turn a hair. I wanted it to get around that I had left town. Kitty would make sure that the word got spread.

It was apple-pie easy stealing the chicken. Baby-bait had been a short-leash idea. A raw chicken would work a treat; they would be so engrossed, tearing it to pieces, they wouldn't notice the ambush. I hid the chicken behind a crate of eggs, figuring that was the last place Mama Mia would look for it. She hit the roof; the air turned purple with Italian profanities. Mexican swear words are red.

Late that night I dragged the carcass across the road. It was smelling pretty high by then. I left it by the entrance to the derelict site. I hoped nobody else would come along. It only needed some fool dog to spoil everything.

I climbed a wall and slid into the shadows, waiting. I chewed on a burger; I never like fighting on an empty stomach. It was a long wait but I was used to waiting. I was used to long nights and lonely nights. It was part of my trade. I stiffened, listening. A can rolled in the wind, a shade shifted, a whiff of odor tainted the air. The ferals were moving.

Two skinny cats crept up on the chicken, tugging it into their territory. Another three came running, tails high, eyes gleaming, and in seconds they were hissing and growling, tearing at the carcass like buzzards. I shuddered to think what would have happened if I had used sweet Kitty as baby-bait. I must have been crazy, out of my marbles.

Suddenly Bruno arrived. He leaped into the fray, throwing cats around like rags, his great yellowed fangs ugly and sour. They ran, howling, some with bits of chicken skin hanging from their jaws.

He slapped a great paw on the mangled corpse and sank his bloodied muzzle into the raw flesh.

I lunged off the wall like an iron wrecking

ball. Fifteen pounds of solid muscle flattened Bruno, knocking all the breath out of him. I sank my teeth into his scrawny neck and he shrieked. Then I fractured his ear for him, embroidered his nose with petit point, kicked a kink into his tail. I wasn't out to kill him, only to reduce him to the sniveling coward that he was, and in front of the other ferals.

But Bruno had some fight left in him. I didn't have it all my own way. He came at me like an odious skunk, biting mean, hitting low. A gash opened over my eye as I staggered back from the onslaught. He was palming blows, coming in with flashing, lightning claws, hind legs drumming into my stomach like a pneumatic drill.

He clamped his jaws on my leg and we rolled over and over in the dust, scrapping, scrawling, biting, scratching. I jerked his face down and put all my weight into a head butt. It knocked him out cold.

Panting, my broad chest heaving, I staggered to my feet and regarded the ring of ferals watching me. My eyes slitted. I was outnumbered, nineteen to one. A low growl came into my throat, warning them not to approach. If I was going out, I was going out blazing.

Suddenly the place erupted. A dozen cats appeared from nowhere and set about the demoralized ferals. It was the local moggies, soft pussy-footers who'd never been in a fight in their lives. Was I glad to see them! They weren't trained in fighting but fury was a fast teacher. The ferals fled.

Bruno left town. No one saw him go. He slunk out at dawn. The rest of the ferals disappeared too. The next day the builders arrived with an earth-digger. It was time for me to move on.

"Ain't yer gonna stay?" said Kitty, licking the wound on my forehead with her soft warm tongue.

"I never stay in one place for long."

"Then I guess you gotta go," she wept.

"I gotta go," I said.

I hitched a lift on a brewer's wagon and rode out of town. I didn't look back. I blinked hard. No one had ever seen the Tooting Bec Cowboy wipe a tear from his eye.

THE
ELECTRIC CAT

Curiosity nearly killed Marcus. It dealt him the monumental fright of his life, singed the tip of his fiery red tail and had him seeing the starriest galaxy.

Marcus was not so much a ginger cat as a red cat. He glowed rust-red and the dense short guard hairs of his undercoat were molten gold. His large eyes were brilliant globes of amber, flecked with inner fire and brimstone. He was ravishingly beautiful, if a male cat can be described in female terms. His family, an ordinary, unremarkable one-child unit, spoilt him to distraction.

He did not enjoy being spoilt, although he would not turn up his eclectic pink nose at Chicken Kiev, Sole Bonne Femme and other

Cordon Bleu delicacies. He was grateful for the sheepskin-lined cosy-cot and twelve-foot-high carpeted scratch pole with random viewing shelves. He even had his own bean bag. He knew he was lucky to live with such kind people, but sometimes he wished they would not try so hard to please him. He liked the odd mangy mouse or flea-ridden bird. And his favorite sleeping place was the old cardboard box under the stairs where they put the jumble.

They were unfortunately a dull family. The woman was boring, the man even more boring, and their pious son the most boredom-inducing member of them all. Marcus could not help wishing wistfully that he lived with a family who had a little more go.

After a particularly boring evening, when the most interesting thing that happened was when Marcus found a leaf stuck to his tail, he decided to stay out all night. A night on the tiles was just what he needed to get his adrenalin going.

So he refused to come in. He crouched in a hedge hideaway, watching the family scurrying round the garden in their nightclothes.

"Marcus, Marcus, Marcus," they called anxiously.

"I know they'll catch him and make him into a fur hat," the woman worried. "He'd make a beautiful hat."

"Munchies, Marcus. Munchies." The son believed in bribery. He wanted to get back to his studies; he had ten thousand words to write on the French Revolution before the weekend.

Marcus did not stir. He wouldn't twitch a

whisker for a Munchie, despite his nightly performance of hopeless addiction. He only did all that purring and pawing to please the woman. She was rather nice, in a boring way.

"Perhaps they've taken him already," she wailed.

"They couldn't catch Marcus," said the man consolingly.

"He can move like lightning. I've seen him."

Those words were to prove prophetic. Quite soon Marcus was to move like lightning; his power would be awesome, an electrostatic phenomenon. He was going to be . . . lit up.

Meantime, Marcus wandered down the garden, the family's calls getting thinner and more frantic. He hardened his heart. If they had played ball with him once, just once, or chased him round the garden or tickled his toes, he would have forgiven them. They fed his body but not his soul. His brain was shriveling; he was on the point of spiritual starvation.

He wandered further than he had ever been before, peering with interest at unknown bushes and fences. There was a strong smell of dog. He leaped a very high fence to show he could still do it and landed smugly; there had been inches to spare despite the extra weight he was carrying.

This is rum, he thought, as he explored the terrain. He was not at all sure that he liked it. The buildings were austere, formidable, functional, clean. There was nothing to play with anywhere. He patted a fire hydrant but it did not respond.

Still the place was different, so that was a point in its favor. He prowled around a room that had a lot of light bulbs and glowing panels flashing in different colors, and a gray machine that whirred and clicked like a typewriter. The room was attractive in a flashy sort of way, but it was empty and could be almost as boring as the family. Nothing was happening.

Marcus slipped through a door which had been left ajar, went down a long flight of concrete stairs and found himself in a huge, cavernous underground room. His spine began to tingle with excitement.

It was as big as a football pitch and contained a row of gigantic machines which looked like metal barrels lying on their sides. The machines were making a deep humming sound which seemed to agitate the concrete beneath Marcus's paws, and he felt his whiskers begin to stir of their own accord. He remembered hearing the son explaining to his parents that the very earliest radios—known as crystal sets—needed no electrical supply other than the tiny fraction of one volt which could be picked up from the sky by an aerial. The key component in one of those primitive radios was a very fine wire, called a cat's whisker, which had a great affinity for electrical forces.

The boring family had yawned at this technical information but Marcus had been fascinated. And now he understood it. He was in a power station ... his whiskers were moving around because the air was full of electricity and they were absorbing it, just as though he were part of a crystal set. It was immense fun and full of possibilities.

The notion that soaking up quantities of electrical energy through his whiskers might be dangerous did not even cross his mind. Marcus had ceased being bored for the first time in ages. He was just about to set off exploring his new adventure playground when he heard footsteps. Determined not to be seen, Marcus took cover beneath one of the huge machines, nesting himself into the massive flanges and bolts which connected it to the floor.

Two men in white coats came hurrying through a doorway.They were carrying clipboards and looked fraught and tense.

"I don't understand it," the taller one said. "We're getting a massive overload. According to the computer this is impossible. It just couldn't happen."

"Never mind the computer," his colleague urged. "The first thing we have to do is find where the—"

His thoughts on what they should look for were never voiced. At that moment there came a cataclysmic explosion, which rocked the floor. Purple sparks fountained through the vast underground room and smoke billowed everywhere. The two men were thrown to the ground as though struck by an invisible force.

A split second later the overloaded machine directly above Marcus spat white-hot metal, and all the electricity it had been producing fought to course down into the earth. But Marcus was in the way. Millions of volts leaped from the machine into his whiskers and from there ran through him like torrents of fire. He did not understand why he did not die instantly. He ought to have died, but by some miracle his whiskers effectively handled the huge surge of power.

Marcus felt as though he was being hurled through a million spinning universes. His body was battered by flaming meteors, huge comets flashed by him dragging their fiery tails, stars exploded with enough violence to light up entire galaxies. Not only his whiskers now, but every red hair on Marcus's body was soaking up unimaginable amounts of electricity.

It was terrifying and yet tremendously exciting.

When it was over, Marcus seemed to return to earth, confused and disoriented. With a raging thirst and a headache, he sank to the floor behind the generator. He thought he would like to go home now. He thought he had had enough excitement for one evening.

The white-coated men staggered to their feet amid the shrieking of sirens and the clamor of alarm bells. The taller one ran to a whirring machine which was like the automatic typewriter Marcus had seen upstairs.

"I can't believe this," he shouted to his companion as he studied the ribbon of paper spilling out of the machine. "The overload has gone! Vanished! Everything is back to normal, thank God."

Marcus slipped out of the great room and went up the stairs. His legs were a little shaky, but he was glad to find that his sense of smell was unimpaired by his extraordinary experience and he was able to retrace his steps to the perimeter fence.

He barely looked at it, even casually. He had jumped it once this evening; there was no reason to expect that he could not jump it again.

He tensed himself for the leap, not realizing that he was thereby concentrating stupendous amounts of electricity in his muscles. A fearsome thunderclap exploded all around him as he sprang into the air. He shot upwards at a terrifying speed.

He was deafened, flattened, compressed and disoriented as lights zig-zagged across his vision, momentarily blinding him. He felt he was spread-eagled across the sky, sucked into the great cosmic blackness of the heavens. Marcus was transfixed with fright. Then just as suddenly it was all over and he found he had landed on the other side of the fence.

Slowly he let the wind out of his cheeks. Very odd, very odd indeed. He stood very still, like a terracotta soldier. It certainly was time he went home. He did not think he could take any more excitement.

He walked stiffly like an old gentleman with arthritis. He had a lot to think about for once.

His usual method of waking each member of the family in the morning was to bounce up and down on their bed, attacking toes, pouncing on ears, patting noses. They always ducked under the duvet and muttered go-away noises.

But this morning the results were most gratifying. Everyone leaped out of bed, shrieking and hopping about, running for cover. The mother locked herself in the bathroom.

Marcus was delighted. He pranced across the landing, swiping at dressing-gown cords and nipping bare feet.

"Ouch!" yelped the father. "What on earth was that? The floor's giving out shocks."

"Perhaps there's a leak, like a gas leak," said the son. Science was not really his strong point. "Or the house needs rewiring."

"Leak . . . whatever do they teach you at that school? It's not common sense, that's for certain. Come on out, Mother. I think it's all over."

"Is it safe?" she quavered from behind the closed door.

"Quite safe. Put the kettle on."

Marcus danced down the stairs ahead of her. Putting the kettle on meant getting the milk out. He was really dry. His throat was quite parched. He twined round the woman's ankles in a gesture of servility. She shrieked and dropped the tea caddy. The kettle hissed steam and overheated. Marcus backed against the refrigerator door and it began to defrost itself. The clock started to go backwards. The microwave switched on its timer and cooked the revolving table.

"Father!" the woman cried. "We're being taken over."

It took nearly twenty minutes for her to heat a small pan of water on an erratic electric cooker with hot plates heating up in no relation to which dials were turned on. The wife moved the pan of water from plate to plate, trying to catch the elusive red coils of heat.

"I'll never cook your breakfast at this rate," she said to Marcus, unaware of the puddle of water that was spreading from under the refrigerator. "It'll have to be a tin."

She put the tin in the electric tin-opener and switched on. It went berserk. The tin spun round at a frantic rate and took the lid off in a flash, then centrifugal force flung out the cat food. Every surface of the kitchen was splashed with Gourmet Fish-Flavored Favorite. The woman had the presence of mind to fall on the off switch. The kitchen walls dripped with mashed fish.

Marcus ran round clearing up for her. This was a lovely way to have breakfast and one he thoroughly approved of. He hoped she'd fling his breakfast all over the kitchen again. Though it was a bit messy . . . his beautiful tail was not meant for mopping up.

She sat down, shaken. "I don't believe it," she said. "I think I'd better get ready for work before anything else happens."

Marcus sat quietly, watching the departure routine. Except it was not quite the same as usual; less boring. The man's electric razor would not work; her heated rollers were on the blink; the son's stereo packed up.

"Put Marcus out."

But no one would touch him. They were not quite sure why, but they were wary. Eventually the son got a broom handle and tried to poke the cat out of the door. Marcus loved it. He parried; he thrust. This was the first time the son had ever played with him. Granted, a broom handle was a bit clumsy; Marcus would have preferred a length of string or a twiggy twig. Still, it was a start. Meanwhile, Marcus managed to bump into the television set and the tube blew, then he tripped over the telephone cord and the entire exchange went out of order.

Once out in the garden, Marcus rushed around to see if anything bad changed overnight. He leaped over the rockery, and . . . wham! Lightning forked the sky with a brilliance that seared the eyeballs.

Marcus caught his breath as he rocketed into the upper air, impelled by enormous voltages, the low-lying clouds vaporizing as he streaked through them. At the peak of his trajectory, he glanced down. The garden was visible as a green postage stamp far below. The family registered as tiny ants, flat on the grass on their stomachs, hands clapped over their ears as peals of thunder split the air.

Marcus fell back to earth, instinctively guiding himself with outstretched forepaws like a sky-diver. He landed accurately on the other side of the rockery, panting. His whiskers were thrumming like piano wires, red fur standing on end. Even his tail was twitching with freak residual currents.

"It's the end of the world," the mother sobbed.

"It's only thunder," said the father.

"I saw our cat up there in the middle of the forked lightning," said the boring son.

Marcus wanted to say goodbye, so he went up

to them in a friendly way; but they ran shrieking to different parts of the garden. Then he had a wonderful time chasing them down the leafy street to the station yard. It was fantastic fun. He couldn't think why no one had thought of it before.

He leaned against a lamp post, catching his breath, and the street-lighting system fused. Most of the cars in the car park overheated and steam poured out of their radiator caps. An electric milk float swerved and a crate of milk fell off, scattering broken milk bottles all over the road. Marcus stood politely on the pavement, eyes glinting. He was so dry again. Sure, it was a terrible thirst he had.

"You want some milk?" asked the milkman, who had a kind heart. "Mind the glass, then."

That evening Marcus went to meet the train. He fancied chasing the family up the street again. He sat on the earthy embankment, watching the evening commuters returning to their homes. It seemed an odd way to spend the day, sitting in trains. A fly buzzed at his nose and Marcus gave an almighty sneeze, blowing leaves in all directions.

The Southern Region signaling system was knocked out in a flash. Trains slowed to a halt. Thief alarms went off in nearby parked cars. It was hours before the couple got home, tired and irritable.

By the end of the week Marcus was banished to sleeping in the jumble box, and he was no longer their "little darling" but "that darned cat." The mother was refusing to cook anything for him. She had to call in the Electricity Board five times to look at the stove and the man was starting to give her funny looks.

"We'll have to get rid of Marcus," said the father.

"But we're not that sort of family," said the mother. "We contribute to all the cat charities."

"I meant we should give him away, not chuck him out on the street."

They put adverts in cat magazines: "Good home wanted for beautiful russet tom (eccentric)."

"You needn't have put in eccentric," the son objected.

"The Trades Descriptions Act," the mother explained.

A lot of people came. Russets were rare. Marcus sat on one of his shelves, looking utterly ravishing with a sweet, docile expression. All went well until he held out his paw politely to have it shaken. Prospective adopters yelped, shrieked, jumped back, fell over and then fled, saying they really wanted a cat that was bigger/smaller/black or with bits of white on it.

"I agree. He'll have to go," said the mother, holding her head in anguish as *Neighbors* stopped transmitting mid-crisis. "I haven't seen a single complete episode this week."

"We could arrange . . . a little accident," said the boring son, who had once read a thriller.

Marcus's sensitive whiskers detected danger.

"Electrocution," the son went on. "In the bath."

Marcus fled. He had had a bath once, after he

had fallen into a slimy pond. Never again. He wasn't going to have another bath even if it killed him.

He leaped out of an open window and ripped open the heavens in a display of sparks and shafts of forked lightning that had the weathermen gasping. He bounced around, traveling at meteoric speeds, not really knowing where to go or what to do. The independence was exhilarating.

"The South of England was blacked out by a freak electrical storm last night which put several power stations out of action and cut off electricity to thousands of homes," said the radio news the next morning. "Weather forecasters say they have never seen anything like it and could not account for the sudden electrical disturbance."

At first Marcus enjoyed being a vagrant. He found an empty shed on a housing estate, and his new friend, the milkman, often gave him milk that was past its drink-by date. But he grew thinner on his mice diet and pined for company. No one would come near him, not even the children. Their mothers pulled them away for fear the cat would harm them.

The milkman felt sorry for the starving cat. "Have some of my breakfast," he said, offering a bite. "My missus makes the scrummiest sausage sandwiches in Surrey, and you should try saying that in a hurry. But no tricks now, young fella. I've had this float in for repairs seven times this month already."

Marcus took especial care to keep his distance. The sausage sandwich was delicious and he was grateful.

As winter came, Marcus became more reclusive and forlorn. Life was not so much fun any more. He was cold and hungry. The family had got themselves another cat to spoil, a haughty black Persian who stared rudely at him from a windowsill. Marcus even crept into the garden and stole the bread they put out for the birds.

To celebrate Christmas, the local Rotary Club decided to organize the biggest Christmas tree ever with thousands of lights sponsored to aid hungry Third World children. People who felt helpless in the face of mass starvation collected money with enthusiasm. The lighting-up would be symbolic.

More than half the population of the town gathered in the square for the lighting-up ceremony. Crowds of children, wrapped in excitement and anoraks, pushed and shoved. Adults, stamping their feet, wondered when they could get to the pub. The organizers peered anxiously at watches as the first flakes of snow began to fall and the temperatures plummeted.

Marcus crept down to the fringe of the crowd, drawn by the cheerful noise. No one spoke to him or touched him. He was totally ostracized by society. He slithered forward, knowing he was unwelcome, but the thought of a dropped chip or morsel of hamburger was too enticing.

He did not walk too well these days. Sleeping rough had brought on arthritis in his back legs. His fur was knotted and tangled from lack of grooming. His ears needed cleaning out and he had a sore on one of his paws that would not heal.

He was only slightly aware that something had gone wrong with the festivities. He was wrapped up in his own chilling misery, lost and alone. The organizers were equally miserable, talking anxiously on portable telephones, pacing the platform under the gigantic tree, refusing to talk to reporters, blocking the television cameras.

A celebrity was waiting for the signal to switch on the lights. She snuggled more deeply into her furs and longed for the promised hospitality to begin.

One of the organizers came to the front of the platform and tapped the microphone. It was dead.

"Ladies and gentlemen! Children!" he shouted. "Unfortunately there has been a power failure and we are unable to begin the ceremony. Blame the cold, the snow, anything. We hope this hiccup won't freeze your generosity in giving to this very worthwhile cause. Stewards will be coming round to you now."

There was a murmur of disappointment from the crowd and people began to drift away. No one was going to hang around on a cold evening looking at an unlit tree. In the confusion, someone trod on Marcus's sore paw.

He shot into the air, clawed through a dark green tunnel smelling of pine, creating a gigantic charge of electricity.

The Christmas tree lit up with a great explosion of light that flooded the town square with brilliance. The crowd shouted with amazement and clapped. It was the most dramatic opening possible.

Marcus sped down from the top of the tree, flickering tongues of light sparking from his fur, trying to find the easiest path to the ground. Suddenly the lights went out, leaving the square cloaked in blackness. Marcus was confused and shaky. Had he been instrumental in providing the light?

He jumped over a litter bin to see what he could do to help.

The crowd roared as the tree lit up again, its myriad lights reflecting the falling snow, turning the square into a twinkling fairyland. Marcus leaped and bounced as the lights flashed on and off.

"Fantastic, brilliant," murmured the star celebrity, accepting a hot rum toddy. "How are you getting all these effects?"

"Trade secret," said the organizer, who did not know either.

Suddenly everyone realized it was Marcus leaping and bouncing around. He was the source of power. The television cameramen fell over each other trying to take shots of him in action, but he was too fast for them.

"That's our cat," said the mother to an admiring throng, totally disregarding the true facts. "That's our Marcus."

"I knew all the time that he was charged with violent electromagnetic radiation," said the boring son to the reporters.

By midnight it was snowing heavily and

strong thoughts of home and hot chocolate dispersed the crowds. The organizers counted the takings. The celebrity had to be helped into a taxi.

Marcus fell exhausted in a heap, a bedraggled bundle, all his energy drained. The lights flickered out. He dragged himself into the shelter of a doorway and blinked away the snowflakes. No one noticed him. He curled up, trying to conserve body heat. A child went to stroke the russet head but his parents pulled him away.

"Don't touch. You might get hurt!"

Well, it had been fun while it lasted, thought Marcus wearily. The best fun in months.

The milkman found Marcus the next morning as he was starting his rounds, a frozen lump of porcupine frosted fur, his inner fire dimmed. He wrapped Marcus in a spare anorak and put him in a milk crate in the driving cab to thaw out. When he had finished his round, he took Marcus home to his missus.

"This is the cat that gives everyone electric shocks," he said, carrying the crate indoors.

"Rubbish," said his wife. "Give him to me. There's nothing wrong with him. Just wants feeding up."

She took the cat on to her lap and stroked his glowing fur. "Fancy a sausage sandwich?" she asked.

She began whizzing round the kitchen in her chair, spinning the wheels expertly, cornering like a racing-track driver. Marcus was amazed. For some reason her legs did not work. She used wheels instead. It took all his agility to keep out of her way.

She put a dish of chopped sausage and gravy down on the floor.

"There you are, young fellow. I'll get something different for you tomorrow. And when you've finished, we'll have a nice game."

She laughed heartily as she began to crunch up silver milk-bottle tops into little round balls. Marcus's amber eyes gleamed. He clenched his paws, quivering, eager to pounce. His red tail swished from side to side. He crouched, shoulders hunched, ears perked, muscles tensed, watching the tantalizing silver balls.

Any second now and he would move like lightning.

About the Author

Stella Whitelaw has had over 150 short stories published in newspapers and women's magazines. She is married with two children and lives in Surrey with her husband and three cats.